THE DELUXE JUNIOR NOVEL

THE DELUXE JUNIOR NOVEL

Based on Characters from DC

Story by
HENRY GAYDEN & DARREN LEMKE

Screenplay by
HENRY GAYDEN

adapted by
CALLIOPE GLASS

SHAZAM! created by
C.C. BECK & BILL PARKER

HARPER
An Imprint of HarperCollins*Publishers*

HARP41771

For information address HarperCollins Children's Books, a division of HarperCollins Publishers, 195 Broadway, New York, NY 10007.
Library of Congress Catalog Number: 2018964868
www.harpercollinschildrens.com
ISBN 978-0-06-289089-4 (hardcover)—ISBN 978-0-06-288417-6 (pbk.)
19 20 21 22 23 PC/LSCH 10 9 8 7 6 5 4 3 2 1
Book design by Erica De Chavez
❖
First Edition

THE DELUXE JUNIOR NOVEL

PROLOGUE

POTOMAC, MARYLAND
DECEMBER 24, 1974

Every year, Thaddeus Sivana begged his mother to let him eat his Christmas Eve dinner alone in his room. And every year she said the same thing.

"Thad, your father works such long hours. He barely gets to see you kids. This is his chance to catch up with you."

And that *sounded* nice, but Thad knew what it actually meant. It meant: *This is his chance to find a new reason to be disappointed in you.*

Thad's father was never disappointed in Thad's big brother, Sid, or in their twin sisters. But Thad was small for his age. He was shy. He was awkward. He wasn't, as his father liked to remind him, a *winner*. He was everything his father hated.

Thad hated Christmas.

But maybe this one won't be so bad, he thought as he reluctantly sat down at the dinner table. For one thing, he'd gotten a really cool present this year—a Magic 8 Ball.

It was heavy in his hand, a glossy black orb with a small round window. It was filled with a cloudy purple liquid. Fortunes came bobbing up through the darkness, murky and wavering until they settled against the clear plastic of the window. Thad could hardly tear his eyes away from it. It felt like magic. Not that magic was real . . . but if it *were* real, this is what it would feel like.

"Thaddeus." Thad's father's voice cut through his daydreaming. Thad jumped a little. "Quit playing with your little toy and sit up straight for once in your life."

Thad glared down at the Magic 8 Ball. It wasn't a *toy*. Toys were for little kids. Toys were fun, harmless things. This—this was practically sorcery.

"He thinks it's *maaaagic*." Thad's older brother, Sid, jabbed him hard in the side. "Geek," he added. Thad's sisters snickered, and Thad hunched over the Magic 8 Ball, refusing to rise to the bait. He shook the ball gently. *Will they leave me alone if I just ignore them?*

An answer drifted up out of the darkness inside the ball.

Don't count on it.

Thad sighed.

"Thad," his mom said. "It's Christmas Eve. You're being rude."

"Sid," Thad's father said, "teach your brother some manners."

Sid stood up and grinned. He pounded one fist into his other palm. "My pleasure, Pop."

He took a step toward Thad.

Thad clutched his Magic 8 Ball and took off running.

⚡⚡⚡

The Sivana family's towering mansion was a maze of rooms and stairs, but in the very center of the house was a large elevator. They'd had it installed when they moved in, for Thad's father, who couldn't walk and used a wheelchair instead.

Sid chased Thad through the west wing of the house and up two flights of stairs to the third floor before Thad had the bright idea of making for the elevator. He ran, his slick church shoes skidding on the antique Persian rug that lined the guest suite hallway. His heart was pounding so hard he thought it might jump right out of his throat. If he could get into the elevator before Sid caught him, Sid would have to double back and use the front staircase. Thad would stand a chance of getting out the front door and up a tree before Sid could make it back down to the first floor.

Thad could hear Sid's heavy footfalls not far behind him as he ran toward the elevator. The doors were still open.

Thad threw himself into the elevator, bouncing off the back wall. He furiously jabbed the "door close" button, and the elevator doors slid shut.

Ding!

The last thing he saw as they closed was Sid's red face, contorted with anger.

He was safe.

Thad hit the button for the first floor and heaved a sigh of relief as he felt the elevator begin to descend.

And descend, and descend.

. . . And descend.

Something was wrong. The elevator should have stopped on the first floor by now, but it was still moving, faster and faster. Mysterious symbols lit up the display, flashing in a sequence too rapid to make out. Thad stared helplessly at the display. Was it a malfunction? Or some kind of special emergency measure? What did those symbols even *mean*? *What was happening?*

The lights went out.

As the elevator continued to plummet, Thad squeezed his eyes shut against the darkness and pressed his back against the elevator wall. He was going to die. He was nine years old and this was the worst Christmas ever and he was going to die right here in this elevator.

And then the elevator slowed to a gentle halt and the doors slid open.

Somehow Thad knew he was far, far from home. He squinted against the light slanting in from a stone chamber. The walls were rough-hewn—it was hard to tell if the space was a cave, or something that had been carved out on purpose. Cautiously, Thad stepped out of the elevator. Behind him, he heard the doors slide shut.

"No!" He turned and lunged for them, but they closed too quickly.

He was stuck here.

Thad turned again and walked slowly into the chamber. On the other end of it, there was a jagged opening—a door. As he approached it, he could see it opened onto a narrow stone bridge. The bridge spanned an apparently bottomless gap about forty feet across. It connected the chamber Thad was in to a stone wall across the gap. Doors lined the stone wall—too many doors to count. The far end of the bridge connected to one of the doors. Thad did the only thing left to do—he stepped forward.

The moment his feet touched the bridge, it detached from the door across the gap and swung out into space. Thad windmilled his arms wildly. He dropped down into a crouch, his heart pounding. He couldn't see the bottom of the gap. What if there *was* no bottom? What if he fell? He looked over his shoulder, wondering if he should crawl back to the door he'd come through . . . but that door had vanished entirely. Thad squeezed his eyes shut. What *was* this place?

The end of the bridge gave a gentle *crunch* as it settled into place against a door several levels higher and farther to the right than the one it had originally led to. Thad scrambled off the bridge and through the door as fast as he could. When he was safe on solid ground, his knees gave out and he collapsed onto the stone floor, panting harshly.

Finally, when Thad's breathing had settled and his heart felt like it might actually stay put in his chest, he raised his head and looked around. His eyes went wide. The space he was in was vast and bewildering. Huge stone columns led up to a vaulted ceiling so high he could barely make it out. There were doors everywhere, and in every shape and size. Some of them were too small even for a cat, and others seemed as though they'd been made for dinosaurs. Set into the wall, scattered among all the infinite doors, were shelves carved out of the rock at chest level, and they were all filled with strange artifacts. In one, a violin burned with an undying flame, yet showed no sign of damage. In another, an eerie green caterpillar-like creature crept across a leaf, tightly caged in a thick glass case. Thad stumbled to his feet and began to make his way through the enormous space, his eyes taking everything in too fast for his brain to process.

"Thaddeus Sivana."

A hoarse voice echoed through the cavernous chamber. Thad jumped a mile. There was someone in there! Barely breathing, he crept forward. Someone was calling him. By name.

Suddenly, it occurred to him: he'd been brought here on purpose. But why? And where *was* he? Thad's thoughts raced as he moved through the space.

And then he saw the old man.

At the far end of the room was a raised dais with seven thrones arranged around its edge in a semicircle. Six of those thrones stood empty, but seated on the seventh was the old man, holding a staff. There was a profound stillness about him. He looked as though he'd been sitting there for centuries—or even longer. His long gray hair swirled around his shoulders. His opulent robe was frayed and crumbling at the edges. Deep creases lined his face, and he had a look of profound weariness . . . and sadness.

But there was power in his form, as well. And sharp eyes undimmed by age peered out at Thad. It was a look that saw everything.

Thad swallowed against the lump of fear in his throat and stepped forward.

"Hello?" he said, his voice shaking. The words seemed to vanish into the cottony, oppressive silence of the temple.

The old man stood, his robe rustling. He took a stiff step forward. Thad stepped back, and began to duck as the old man raised his staff. But the bolt of power that emerged from it never reached Thad. Instead, it lit up the air between them, carving a holographic scene out of nothing.

Thad stared, transfixed. He traced his fingers through the image—it looked so *real*. But his hand swept through empty air.

The moving image showed a great battle taking place. Seven mighty Wizards locked in desperate combat against seven demons. Each Wizard seemed to have a different power. Speed, strength, flight, lightning . . . they used their different strengths in concert with one another, moving with the fluidity of a practiced team—or a family.

One of the Wizards looked familiar. Thad watched him closely, until suddenly he understood what he was seeing: it was the old man! But he was younger in this image, his face unlined and his movement easy and powerful as he fought his way past a wall carved with hieroglyphics. Thad squinted. Was that . . . were they fighting in *ancient Egypt*? How old *was* this guy?

"I am sole survivor of the Council of Wizards," the old man said, as though answering Thad's unspoken question. "For ages we protected humankind from the Seven Deadly Sins."

Thad watched the ghostly image as the Wizard and his six comrades continued their battle against the seven demons—the Seven Deadly Sins. He shivered. Inky waves of evil power rippled off the Sins, distorting the air around them like a country road on a hot day. Thad watched as slowly, agonizingly, the tides of war turned against the Sins.

But the Sins gave as good as they got—one by one, the Wizards were wounded in battle, some of them very badly.

As the Sins fell, the Wizards began to fall, too.

When the last Sin was defeated, the Wizard and his dying comrades locked them, one by one, into huge, grotesque stone statues.

"At last we subdued them," the Wizard continued. "But at terrible cost. Six of my brothers and sisters fell in the battle. I alone remain."

The image faded and vanished. The Wizard sighed, weariness wrapped around him like a cloak. "Countless years have passed since that time. I grow weak. I seek a Champion to inherit my power."

He fixed Thad with a keen stare. Thad's breath caught in his throat.

"You want . . . to give me magic?" he choked out.

The Wizard raised his staff again. "I will transfer my powers to you with this," he said. "But first I must know that you are strong in spirit . . . and pure of heart."

As the Wizard spoke, a muffled whisper reached Thad's ears. At first a single voice, then another, until a chorus of spiteful, hissing words—just quiet enough that Thad couldn't make them out—had wrapped itself around the room. The sound was soft, but there was something insistent about it. It refused to be ignored. It felt like the whispers were reaching into Thad's head somehow.

Where were the voices *coming* from? Thad looked around the throne room and noticed, for the first time, a row of grotesque statues along one wall. There were seven of them, each uglier than the last. They were the statues from the Wizard's story . . . the prisons of the Seven Sins.

"Only the most worthy . . . ," the Wizard began, but the voices rose in a chorus and drowned out the rest of his sentence.

Thaddeus, they hissed. The hair on the back of Thad's neck stood up.

Thaddeus Sivana.

Ignored.

Overlooked.

Scorned.

Bullied.

We see you.

We see your potential.

We see your worth.

Ignore this weak old man.

We can give you true power.

"Fight them, Thaddeus! True power comes from your best self, not from the Seven Deadly Sins." The Wizard's voice, an urgent plea, filtered through the whispers. But it was muffled and distant, as though it was coming from a long way away.

Thad turned away from the Wizard.

He *was* ignored. Overlooked. Bullied.

He was powerless. *Everyone* had power over him. His father, his mother, Sid. The other kids at school, who laughed at him. The teachers, who said he was too distracted, too timid, to ever amount to anything. Being pure of heart wouldn't solve any of his problems. Being powerful *would.*

Thad swallowed hard and walked away from the Wizard, toward the statues. They seemed somehow to move without moving, their eyes showing an eerie intelligence. A pedestal carved with ancient symbols stood in front of them. Glowing atop the pedestal was an orb, about the size of his Magic 8 Ball. It radiated power and menace . . . and Thad knew he had to have it.

As he approached, the Sins' whispers crescendoed into a deafening roar.

Take the orb, they screamed.

Free us!

Thad reached his hand toward the orb, and just as his fingers were about to touch it, the world spun, and a crashing blow drove the breath out of Thad's lungs. Everything went perfectly black, and perfectly silent, for just a moment.

When he opened his eyes again, gasping for breath, Thad was sprawled on the floor halfway across the chamber, and the orb sat untouched on its pedestal.

The Sins' voices were silent, the statues cold and motionless. And the Wizard stood over Thad, his face fierce and hard.

"What . . . happened?" Thad gasped. His head was spinning, and his whole body ached.

"The power of the Council of Wizards is only for the pure of heart," the Wizard said coldly. "You, Thaddeus Sivana, are no Champion after all."

"But—" Thad began. But the Wizard raised his staff.

"Begone," he said, and brought it down in a single arc of light.

⚡⚡⚡

Ding!

The elevator doors closed against Sid's red face, contorted with anger.

Thad looked around wildly as the elevator began to descend. It was like his life had been rewound somehow—he was back where he'd started. How was that possible? He staggered into the corner, his heart pounding. Did this mean he was going to get another chance? Another opportunity to make the right decision and become the Wizard's Champion?

The elevator continued to descend. But this time no ancient symbols illuminated the display panel. Instead, the elevator gave a cheerful little chime as it passed the second floor. The elevator wasn't going anywhere except the first floor of the Sivana mansion, where Sid was currently hurrying so he could beat the pulp out of Thad.

"No!" Thad screamed. He'd had his chance and he'd lost it. Despair choked him.

"Please! Let me back in! It isn't fair! Let me have it!" He pounded on the walls. "Please!"

Ding!

The elevator doors slid open at the first floor. Sid skidded down the hall and slid to a stop in front of Thad, fists raised and a mean grin on his face.

"Ha! Get ready for a—"

"Let me have it!" Thad screamed at everybody and nobody, desperation sweeping over him. Sid lowered his arms, confusion washing across his face, but Thad hardly

noticed. He turned in a frantic circle, and his elbow clipped Sid's face, hard.

Sid stared at Thad, shocked, and touched his cheekbone. His fingers came away bloody.

He attacked.

Sid's first blow caught Thad under the chin, snapping his head back. Thad lost his footing, and the moment he hit the floor, Sid kicked him in the stomach.

Thad curled into a tight ball, sobbing in pain and humiliation. The Magic 8 Ball fell from his hand and rolled a few slow feet until it stopped, wobbling, windowpane up. Thad reached for it.

"You know what?" Sid said, stepping on Thad's hand just hard enough to bring tears to his eyes. "It's Christmas, and I'm feeling generous."

He lifted his foot and walked away. "Enjoy your stupid toy, loser."

Thad lay on the floor, gasping for breath, clutching his stomach.

"It isn't fair," he whispered. He'd been *so close*, so close to being someone. So close to mattering.

So close to having *power*.

After what felt like an eternity, Thad pushed himself up to sit, slumped against the wall next to the elevator. He stared dully at the Magic 8 Ball.

Outlook not so good, it said.

Yeah, Thad thought. *No kidding.*

But then the letters began to shift and swim. Thad blinked hard, and they rearranged themselves into a new message:

Find us.

The words faded after a moment, but Thad didn't need to see them anymore. He knew he would never forget them.

He would find the Sins. He would free them. He would take their power. And when he did . . .

The Wizard would be sorry. Sid would be sorry.

The whole world would learn to fear Thaddeus Sivana.

CHAPTER 1

In the echoing silence of the Rock of Eternity, the Wizard lowered himself onto his throne. Countless centuries of age were weighing on him more heavily than ever. And each potential Champion that he summoned seemed to be worse than the last one.

The latest . . . Thaddeus? Had that been his name? The Wizard shook his head. It didn't matter. The boy hadn't hesitated for a moment before falling prey to the Sins' temptations. A failure, just like all the others.

Would he never find a Champion?

Summoning up his strength, the Wizard began the

incantation again. Perhaps this time the candidate who arrived would truly be worthy.

PHILADELPHIA, PENNSYLVANIA
TODAY

"Boy, am I glad to see you guys!" fourteen-year-old Billy Batson cried as the squad car squealed into the strip mall parking lot. Two police officers emerged from the car, and Billy hurried up to them. "I called nine-one-one as soon as I saw what was going on. I just couldn't stand by and let this happen!"

He pointed to the pawnshop. Its door stood ajar, lock picks still hanging from the lock. The alarm blared. "They're in there!" Billy said earnestly.

"Thanks, kid," one of them said, not taking his eyes from the open door of the shop. The two cops moved cautiously toward it. "We'll take it from here."

"Police!" the other one yelled into the shop. "Come out with your hands up!"

"They're hiding in the closet in the back!" Billy added helpfully.

As the police moved into the pawnshop, Billy trailed after them.

"Gosh, be careful in there!" he called as he collected

his lock picks and pulled down the steel grate, snapping the padlock closed around its latch. "There sure are some bad people in this city!"

Click.

The cops turned around at the sound of the padlock, and Billy gave them a friendly grin. "You just can't trust anyone these days, am I right?"

"Hey!" one of them yelled as the other rattled the grate. They were locked in tight.

Billy winked at the cops and sauntered over to the squad car. Its doors were still open. Too easy. Billy rolled his eyes. They fell for it every time.

The squad car was still warm inside. Billy shut the doors and settled into the driver's seat, enjoying the heat. His threadbare jacket and worn-out shoes didn't help keep out the cold and slush of a Philadelphia winter. It felt like he'd been cold for days. Because, come to think of it, he *had* been cold for days.

But he had pressing business. Ignoring the enticing smell of the two fresh cheesesteak sandwiches sitting on the dashboard, Billy got to work. He pulled a notebook from his battered backpack and opened it to the last page, skimming down the list of crossed-out names until he got to the very last one.

"Batson, Batson, Batson," he muttered, tracing his finger down the page. All of them had been dead ends. But this last one—

"Aha. Rachel Batson."

Billy had a good feeling about this one.

He pulled up a new search in the squad car's mobile data terminal and began looking for an address for Rachel Batson.

Bingo.

Grabbing the sandwiches as he left the car, Billy waved goodbye to the cops.

"Sorry, boys!" he called. "Nothing personal."

Billy dug into one of the sandwiches as soon as he got a seat on the subway. Why wait? They were warm, and he was starving.

One sandwich was down the hatch and Billy was about to start on the other one when he saw her. The homeless woman was slumped in a seat across the train from him, staring blankly at the floor. She looked tired, dirty, and sad. She also looked really, really hungry. Billy looked at the paper-wrapped sandwich in his hand. Sure, this was his first really good meal in a while, but his hunger was nothing compared to that of someone living rough on the street. He knew from past experience. And this was his stop, anyway.

Billy handed the second sandwich to the woman as he left the train.

Without the sandwich distracting him, Billy couldn't stop thinking about where he was going. Rachel Batson's house wasn't far from the subway stop, but the walk felt endless. He practiced his introduction as he walked.

"Hey, let me introduce myself. I'm Billy Batson." No, that made him sound like a con man.

"I've been looking for you, Rachel." He grinned winningly at his reflection in a store window, but it didn't help: now he sounded like a serial killer.

Billy scowled at himself. He kind of *looked* like one, too. He took a moment to finger-comb his dark hair into submission, but there wasn't much he could do about the dark circles under his eyes or the chalky tinge of his pale skin. And his clothes were beyond worn-out. He'd just have to live with looking like what he was: a runaway foster kid with a couple of cheesed-off, hungry cops on his trail.

Billy kicked a stone down the sidewalk ahead of him and kept walking. He was as close as he'd ever been, but this was also the last name on his list. It had to be her. It *had* to. There was no one left.

He tried again.

"Hi, Mom."

⚡⚡⚡

When Billy Batson was five years old, he lost his mom.

When most people say they lost their mom, it's just a gentler way of saying their mom died. Billy had spent the last nine years of his life explaining to people that he meant it literally: he'd *lost his mom.* They'd been at the winter carnival together, fighting their way through the crowd to the Ferris wheel. One moment his mother was there . . .

And the next minute, Billy was alone in a swirling crowd of people. The cops had promised she'd come find him. But days had passed, then weeks, then years, and Billy's mom hadn't appeared.

So Billy went looking for *her*.

And eventually, he'd tracked down almost every woman between the ages of twenty-eight and forty with the last name of Batson in the state of Pennsylvania. He'd met career women and housewives, rich people and poor people, and, on one especially terrifying day, a tattooed lion tamer. Some of them were kind, and some of them were suspicious and unfriendly. The kind ones were, somehow, harder to talk to. But none of them were his mother.

Billy kept trying. Year after year he continued his search . . . until there was just one person left on his list.

One last chance.

⚡⚡⚡

The house was a tidy row house on a nice residential street.

Billy's heart started pounding harder and harder as he walked up to the front door. Hastily wiping his sweaty palms on his pants, he rang the bell.

"Yes?" a woman's voice called through the closed door.

"Rachel Batson?" Billy asked, his voice shaking. He cleared his throat.

"Who's asking?" the voice replied.

"I—okay, I know this sounds crazy, but I think you're my mom," Billy said in a rush.

There was a startled silence, and then Rachel Batson opened the door. She was a tall woman with a kind face, a keen stare, and mahogany-brown skin.

Billy's heart sank.

She quirked an eyebrow at Billy and looked him up and down with a pointed expression. "Oh, really?" she said.

"My mistake," Billy said quietly. Behind him, a siren wailed. Billy turned.

"I could have forgiven being locked in a pawnshop," the cop said, stepping out of the car. "But then you had to go and take our lunch."

CHAPTER 2

Billy's file at Child Protective Services was the size of a phone book. He was kind of proud of that, actually. But he still winced when it hit Ms. Glover's desk with a resounding *wham*.

"Ran away again, I see," she said.

"You sending me back?" Billy asked, although to be honest, he didn't really care one way or another. Foster homes were all the same anyway. Well, not exactly: there was the old lady who made all her foster kids knit scarves so she could sell them as "artisanal neck cozies" on Etsy and pocket the profits. Then there was the conspiracy theorist who wouldn't stop talking about the Lizard People—he even made picture books about them so the youngest kids in the group home wouldn't feel left out. And Billy's favorite had been the couple who spent all their government checks on ceramic cat figurines . . . instead of food for the kids. Billy had eaten toast for every meal for two weeks before he ran away that time.

So they weren't all *exactly* the same, but they had one thing in common: they all stunk.

"They don't want you back," Ms. Glover said plainly. Billy snorted.

"You laugh," she said darkly, "but you've run away from foster homes all over the state. From people who want you. All in pursuit of someone who clearly does *not*. Kid," Ms. Glover continued, her voice suddenly gentle, "your mother doesn't want to be found."

And there it was. The truth Billy had been denying his whole life.

"There is a couple who run a group home here in Philadelphia," Ms. Glover said quietly. "They're waiting outside."

Billy looked out into the hallway. A woman with kind eyes looked back at him. She had shoulder-length dark hair and a pretty face, and her expression was warm. The big guy standing next to her nodded at Billy.

"You are out of options, Mr. Batson," Ms. Glover said. "Don't screw this up."

⚡⚡⚡

Billy's new group home was run by Rosa and Victor Vasquez. They'd been fostering kids for a long time—and they'd both been foster kids themselves. They laid it out for Billy as they headed back to the group home.

"I'd been in the system since I was four," Victor explained from behind the wheel of the van.

"And I was in and out starting around ten," Rosa added. She smiled at Victor. "That's actually how we met—we ended up at the same group home when we were both seventeen."

"No idea what she saw in me," Victor said, grinning ruefully at Billy in the rearview mirror. "I was a mess."

"Yeah," Rosa said, poking Victor affectionately in the side, "a mess with a heart of gold."

Billy rolled his eyes. Outside the van window, they passed old houses with big trees out front. It wasn't a fancy neighborhood, but it wasn't scary, either. The van slowed to a stop on a quiet side street.

"Here it is," Victor said, gesturing grandly at a run-down

old house. A string of half-burned-out Christmas lights flickered where they'd been carefully draped across the edge of the roof. "The perfect home. Just needs a fresh coat of paint, new wiring, new roof, new walls, new floors . . . You know, little tweaks." He grinned at Billy.

Despite himself, Billy smiled. It was nice of Victor to make the effort to be funny. He didn't realize that the effort was wasted—Billy wouldn't be staying. But Victor didn't need to know that yet. He'd find out soon enough.

The house was a mess, but a cheerful one. The worn furniture looked comfortable. There were books and CDs on the shelves, on the tables, and scattered here and there on the couch and floor. A messy crafts project had taken over part of a side table, and there was a half-completed jigsaw puzzle on the floor in the entryway.

"We're home!" Rosa said loudly. But although Billy could hear muffled K-pop playing upstairs, there weren't any other signs of life. Rosa sighed. Billy wondered if she'd been expecting someone, or something, to appear.

"Take the kill! Now, now, now!" someone yelled in the next room. Billy froze for a moment, alarmed, before he saw Rosa roll her eyes.

"It's just Eugene," she explained.

Eugene turned out to be a kid a few years younger

than Billy, playing a video game in the living room. He had headphones on and didn't seem to notice when they entered the room.

"Not much of a welcome party," Rosa said apologetically.

A half-completed "Welcome Home, New Brother" banner was strewn across a sofa, abandoned in a pool of glitter. As they walked into the dining room, where the table was half-set, the kitchen door burst open and a tiny little girl with a manic gleam in her eye and glitter all over her clothes came bustling out carrying a huge pot. She placed it hastily on the table and threw herself at Billy.

"Hi," she said, hugging him hard. Billy stared down at the top of her head, at a complete loss. What was he supposed to do? Hug her back? Billy hadn't hugged anyone in nearly a decade. He wasn't planning on starting now. But she wasn't letting go, and he had a feeling she wasn't going to until he did *something*. Finally, he patted her head awkwardly.

Rosa smiled. "Darla, meet your new brother, Billy. Billy, this is Darla."

Darla finally let go, and grinned up at Rosa. "We've met," she said. Billy looked down at himself. He was covered in glitter.

A teenaged girl talking seriously on a cell phone wandered by. "No, but that's what makes your math department so perfect for me," she said earnestly. She muted the phone briefly and caught Billy's eye. "Welcome," she said. "Sorry about this, but my entire future is riding on this call."

"Mary's doing a college interview," Rosa explained to Billy.

"Mention you're a foster kid," Victor said to Mary. "They'll love that." Mary flashed Victor a thumbs-up and unmuted the phone. "I'm glad your campus is so inclusive," she said to the person on the other end of the line. "As a foster child, found family is so important to me."

She wandered away, still chattering confidently into the phone.

"Where are Freddy and Pedro?" Rosa asked Darla. Darla winced. "The glitter triggered Pedro's asthma," she said, "and he freaked out and locked himself in his room. Freddy's upstairs, probably researching Kryptonian exobiology or something."

Darla turned to Billy, and her face lit up eagerly. "Freddy's so smart," she said. "You're going to love him. I bet you guys end up best friends—just like brothers should be!" She smiled winningly. Billy didn't smile back.

"Come on," Rosa said. "I'll show you your room."

Billy slung his backpack over his shoulder, and they started up the stairs. "Watch the bum step," Rosa said, steering Billy to the side as a kid a year or two older than him thudded down past them, K-pop blasting in his headphones.

"Pedro," Rosa said, "this is Billy."

Pedro nodded shyly, not taking off his headphones. He hurried on down the stairs.

Billy's room was on the second floor, at the end of the hallway. "You'll be sharing with Freddy," Rosa said. She stuck her head in. "Freddy, this is Billy Batson. Try not to freak him out *immediately*, okay?"

She smiled encouragingly at Billy and shooed him into the room. "See you at dinner, boys," she said, and then she was gone and Billy was standing in his new room. It was too bad the room was on the second floor—that would make it harder to sneak out the window in the middle of the night. Ignoring the kid—Freddy—sitting at the desk, Billy moved toward the windows to see if there were any convenient tree branches or fire escapes he might be able to use.

"Yeah, it's quite a drop," Freddy said. He stood up, using a crutch to lever himself out of the chair. "I should know."

That didn't sound good. Billy turned and raised an eyebrow.

"Victor threw me out that window," Freddy explained. "That's how . . ." He gestured at his crutch and his leg to finish the sentence.

Billy's mind went blank. Victor? He'd struck Billy as naive but harmless . . .

Freddy nodded, his face serious. "They *act* perfectly nice," he said, "but don't be fooled."

Billy's head spun. What kind of home *was* this?

Then Freddy dissolved into laughter and clapped Billy on the shoulder. "Joke!" he said. Billy heaved a sigh of relief. But if that wasn't why Freddy used a crutch, then what *was* the reason?

"It's actually a terminal disease," Freddy explained, suddenly grave. "I'll be dead within months. You can have my stuff when I go."

Billy stared at him, feeling like he'd been thrown into a washing machine on spin cycle. Was he serious? Laughing at a dying kid was kind of beyond the pale, even for Billy. But what if he was—

"Gotcha!" Freddy said, grinning. "I know, you look at me and you're like, 'Why so dark? You're a disabled kid in foster care! You've got it all!'"

Billy couldn't help it—he laughed. This kid was weird, but Billy kind of liked him. What was his deal anyway? Billy looked around the room, trying to get a sense of who Freddy was. The room was messy—the bottom bunk of the bunk bed unmade, with sheets and blankets dripping onto the floor. Billy noted that the top bunk had been neatly made up with a fluffy comforter and a crisp set of sheets. That was where they thought he'd be sleeping, he guessed. The rest of the room was a combination of the usual teenage-boy stuff—an old TV, messy piles of comic books, a keyboard synthesizer leaning against one wall, that sort of thing—and a truly impressive super hero paraphernalia collection.

Framed news articles about Superman, Batman, and the rest of the Justice League hung on the walls. Freddy's desk was cluttered with stacks of thick, serious-looking books about super heroes and society, super hero biology, super heroes and philosophy, you name it. There were a few pretty high-end action figures, about fifty million commemorative Superman cups, and—Billy's eyes went wide—a *very* real-looking Batarang.

"Is that—" Billy started, moving closer to examine it.

"A replica, alas," Freddy answered. "But isn't it cool? Feel how sharp it is. I could totally kill you with this thing.

But I won't!" he added hastily. "Since we need you for our team of international jewel thieves."

Billy didn't blink. He was beginning to get used to Freddy's wild yo-yo-ing style of conversation. Freddy continued without missing a beat, "I'm more of a Superman fan, personally. I keep my best stuff in here. Check it out. . . ."

He slid open his desk drawer, revealing a pile of newspaper clippings, scribbled notes, computer printouts, and, in a small plastic baggie, a misshapen piece of metal about the size and shape of a smashed blueberry. An official-looking little card with the words CERTIFICATE OF AUTHENTICITY printed on it sat in the baggie alongside the metal blob.

Freddy held it up, reverence on his face. "Behold," he said, "a nine-millimeter bullet, shot at Superman himself. It's real. And it's probably worth seven or eight hundred dollars."

Billy's ears perked up at that. He could *really* use seven or eight hundred dollars. He took another look at that desk drawer. No lock. Good.

"Anyway, if you're gonna be in foster care," Freddy went on obliviously, "you could do a lot worse. Victor and Rosa are super chill. You lucked out with this placement."

Billy nodded absently. "Sure," he said. "Bathroom?"

"Oh! Uh, down the hall," Freddy said, pointing.

"Got it," Billy said, walking out the door.

Billy locked the bathroom door behind him and sat down on the toilet lid, suddenly exhausted. It had been a long, long day. He opened his notebook and stared at the list of crossed-out names, with *Rachel Batson* sitting hopefully at the bottom. He fished around in his backpack until he found a pen, and carefully drew a line through it.

Now what? he thought.

"Dinner!" Victor's voice filtered up through the heating register.

Without letting himself think twice about it, Billy crammed his notebook into the small trash can and headed downstairs.

CHAPTER 3

"There were seven," Kathy Yates said. Her face on the computer screen was pale and anxious.

"Seven statues. Whispering. And then, *zip*—" she continued. "I was back in my apartment."

Dr. Lynn Crosby frowned and made a note in her file. "Thank you, Ms. Yates," she said, speaking to the woman via the video call on the computer in front of her. Behind her in the research center's computer lab, a tall, bald man stood watching her conduct the video interview. He toyed idly with a black plastic sphere.

Dr. Thaddeus Sivana still had that Magic 8 Ball, after all

these years. And after all these years, he was still searching—still looking for a way back into the Rock of Eternity. A path back to the Wizard . . . and the Seven Deadly Sins. He'd funneled all his resources into this research program, locating and interviewing other people who had been summoned—and rejected—by the Wizard. He'd had to do a certain amount of lying in the process—his employees all thought they were researching a mass hallucination, not a real phenomenon. But Sivana didn't mind lying.

After all, it had been made quite clear to him at a young age that he'd never be pure of heart.

"No one would listen to me," Kathy Yates went on, her tinny voice reverberating through the research center. "But I know it was real."

Dr. Crosby swung the camera mounted on the computer so it faced a table in the research center. On the table was a scale model of the ancient stone temple.

"Is this what you saw?" Dr. Crosby asked the woman.

Astonishment swept across her face. "Are you saying this has happened to other people?" she gasped.

"Well, kind of," Dr. Crosby replied. "Reoccurring themes like this are frequent in cases of mass hysteria." She held up a sheet of paper with seven symbols drawn on it.

"Do you recall seeing these?" she asked. Behind her,

Sivana's gaze sharpened, and he leaned forward. Kathy Yates looked doubtfully at the symbols.

"No . . . ," she said, and Sivana hung his head. Another dead end. Countless interviews—countless victims of the Wizard's cruel tricks—and he was still no closer to unlocking the method of opening a portal to the Rock of Eternity. He turned and started for the door. Dr. Crosby could complete the interview on her own—he was no longer interested in observing.

"But I've got video," Kathy Yates added. "You can see the door lighting up!"

Now, *that* was interesting. Sivana spun around and crossed the room in a few long strides. He leaned urgently into the camera, cutting off Dr. Crosby.

"Show it to me," he said.

The video that popped up on the screen was shaky, but Sivana could clearly see the digital alarm clock next to the door flashing a familiar sequence of symbols . . . seven times.

Dr. Crosby caught up to Sivana as he strode toward his office.

"Countless confirmed encounters," he said to himself, "and I didn't see it. Until now."

"What?" Dr. Crosby said. Sivana closed his office door in her face. But she stuck her foot in, blocking it from latching. Fine. Sivana didn't care—the world would know soon enough anyway. Let her find out a few minutes before everyone else. He approached the door he'd placed standing in its frame in the center of his office.

"All this time . . . ," Sivana muttered, beginning to draw the now-familiar sequence of symbols on the door. "And the important part was to repeat the sequence *seven times*."

One.

He kept drawing.

Two.

"Are you kidding?" Dr. Crosby demanded incredulously. Sivana shook his head, not looking up.

Three.

"What these people . . . ," he said, drawing the sequence again—

Four.

". . . have been experiencing . . ."

Five.

". . . really happened."

Six.

"You really *believe* this?" Dr. Crosby said scornfully.

She slapped her hand against the door in punctuation.

Seven.

The door flashed bright just as Dr. Crosby's hand hit it. Faster than Sivana could track it, the blinding light bled from the door into her fingers and up her arm.

She was obliterated in a flash.

"As a matter of fact," Sivana said cheerfully to the spot where Dr. Crosby had been standing only a moment before, "I do."

He watched, hardly daring to hope, as the door swung slowly open. On the other side . . .

On the other side lay the Rock of Eternity. The ancient temple he'd been chasing his entire life. The obsession he'd been driven by since he was a furious, heartbroken nine-year-old.

The means to his revenge against the entire world.

Sivana stepped through the door.

The seven statues imprisoning the Seven Sins were still there, but cracks had begun to show in the stone. Sivana supposed that as the Wizard's power waned, the Sins were beginning to break through . . . slowly, slowly. Well, he would help speed that up.

The Wizard was still there, too—still sitting on the

same throne, even. It was as though he hadn't moved in forty years. But Sivana knew that couldn't be true—the Wizard had been busy in the meantime. Busy summoning candidate after candidate. Every time, holding out the hope of power beyond imagination . . . and then dashing that hope to the ground.

The Wizard still hadn't found his Champion. And now he never would. Not if Sivana had anything to say about it.

As Sivana stepped into the temple, the Wizard looked up, startled—alarmed.

"I've been waiting for this moment for so long," Sivana said. The Wizard stared at him, his old eyes peering keenly, poring across Sivana's face.

"You don't recognize me," Sivana said, realizing. "I suppose that makes sense. You've brought countless people here, all in hopes of finding someone *perfect*." He spat the word out with all the scorn it deserved.

"I remember you," the Wizard rasped. He'd aged even more in the last forty years. His hand shook as he raised his staff. "A disappointment."

"Imagine for a moment," Sivana said, fury rising inside him, "what it's like to hear that from *everyone*, your *entire life*?" He stalked forward, and the Wizard rose, trembling, out of his throne, his staff held aloft.

"But you were right about one thing," Sivana added thoughtfully, "I'm not *good*. I know that now. I don't *need* to be good. I just need to be *powerful*." He turned from the Wizard and moved toward the orb, still glowing on its platform, still protected by a powerful force field. But now Sivana knew the combination. He rearranged the symbols on the plinth in the same sequence as he'd written on the door, and the force field abruptly deactivated. The subsonic hum it had been emitting went suddenly quiet. And the silence in the temple seemed somehow even more profound as Sivana reached out and took the Eye of Sin.

"*No!*" the Wizard cried. But it was too late. Unseen locks sprang open, and the seven statues crumbled.

Instantly, seven wraiths flowed from the rubble of the statues in a cloud of unctuous, smoky mist. They formed themselves into seven twisted, grotesque figures, standing behind Sivana as he faced the Wizard.

One of them—Wrath—oozed forward. "You still don't have a Champion," he hissed at the Wizard. "But now *we do*." One by one the Sins swept into the Eye, which now floated above Sivana's outstretched palm. He watched in sick fascination as the shades were sucked in. When all seven had entered the Eye, it rose farther into the air, and then—before Sivana could move or even cry out—the Eye of Sin shrank down to the size of a human eye, flew toward him, and buried itself in his own eye socket!

For a moment, the pain was unbearable. It felt as though a hot poker had been thrust into his head. But quickly the pain turned into a rush of power. The Sins were *inside* him now.

Thad.

Thaddeus Sivana.

Our Champion.

Seeker of revenge.

Use our power.

It is yours now.

Show your family . . .

Show the world.

The Sins' ugly whispers had become a part of his own thoughts. And as Wrath moved to the front, Sivana felt his mind fill with raw anger. It felt good.

"Fight them!" the Wizard cried. He thrust his staff forward, flinging a lightning bolt toward Sivana. "They're just using you—to destroy mankind!"

Sivana instinctively brought his arms up to shield his face from the bolt of lightning searing through the air toward him. But as he did it, new power coursed through him and captured the bolt in a field of energy.

Hmm. That *was an interesting development.*

"Maybe," Sivana said, raising his head, "mankind has it coming. We're all murderers and thieves, in one way or another. You want someone pure of heart? Good luck."

He focused his new power on the Wizard, adjusting to the eerie double vision of his human eye and the Eye of Sin. He could still see through his remaining natural eye. But now he could also see the world through the Eye of Sin. Seen through the orb, things looked warped and dark and somehow dirtier.

Black lightning arced toward the Wizard in a furious barrage, striking him again and again, flinging his body back toward the seven empty, crumbling thrones. He fell, wounded and nearly unconscious.

"No . . . ," he whispered, but Sivana had already turned his back. There was nothing more for him here. The Wizard had tasted his power . . . and his anger.

Now it was the world's turn.

CHAPTER 4

Alone again in the Rock of Eternity, the Wizard slumped to the floor. His wounds were grievous, and black rot spread from them to every corner of his body. He didn't have long left, and he knew it.

The Wizard gathered his strength and cast the searching spell one last time.

"Find me one soul who is worthy," he breathed.

Surely, surely such a one must exist.

Billy waited until the rest of the house was sound asleep before he pulled back the covers, grabbed his backpack, and made his way quietly downstairs. The front hallway was dark—the only light was from a streetlamp outside, shining in through the window by the door.

"You aren't wasting any time, are you?" The voice startled him badly, and Billy jumped. It was Mary, her face carefully blank. "I didn't like it here, either, at first," she continued gently, and Billy rolled his eyes. He continued on his way to the door. A small red light flashed on a panel by the doorframe. An alarm. Great. He'd have to disable it before he could get out. Well, he knew how to do that. He rummaged in his backpack for the mini–tool kit he took with him everywhere.

"Do you even have a plan?" Mary asked.

"I can take care of myself," Billy said flatly. "Hey!"

Mary plucked the kit from his hands and slipped it into her back pocket. Billy sighed. Time to try a different tactic. He pasted a rueful expression onto his face.

"Look," he said, scratching his head bashfully. "You seem really nice. Rosa and Victor seem really nice. It's not that I'm not grateful. It's just hard for me to trust people, you know? But I guess I can give it a try." He held out his hand for a handshake. "Tell you what: I'll stick around, and you don't tell anyone about this . . . little mistake. Deal?"

Mary shook his hand, and then grabbed his *other* hand, which had been slipping around to nab his tool kit out of her back pocket.

"Busted," Mary said. Billy bristled. He was an *excellent* pickpocket.

"I must be having an off night," he muttered.

"Just give this place a chance," Mary said seriously. "People can surprise you sometimes."

She held her hand out, and in it was—Billy's wallet? Billy patted his pants pocket frantically. Sure enough, his wallet wasn't there. Mary was *good.* He looked at her with newfound respect.

"We're all foster kids here," Mary said. "Now go back to bed." She pointed imperiously up the stairs.

Billy went. He knew when he was beat.

⚡⚡⚡

Fawcett Central School looked like a prison. Billy eyed it doubtfully as he trailed behind the rest of Victor and Rosa's pack of foster kids. A huge crowd of students streamed into the building. *Fellow inmates,* Billy thought to himself.

"It's a big school," Darla said, noticing Billy's gaze. "You may be thinking, *Wow, look at all these strangers.* But not if you see them as future friends! Then it's like, *Wow, look at all these friends!*"

She grinned sweetly up at Billy.

"Is she for real?" Billy asked Mary as they were swept along into the school by the crowd.

"Never doubt it," Mary said. "Darla's basically a unicorn in human form. I think her heart pumps glitter instead of blood. Also, she basically never stops talking."

"Silence makes me uncomfortable!" Darla chirped. "I cope with the trauma of my uprooted personal history by keeping up a steady stream of inconsequential conversation!" She winked cheerfully at Billy. Freddy held up his hand for a high five, and Darla slapped his palm enthusiastically. "That's the spirit," he said.

Ahead of them, two bro-ish guys who were obviously twins turned around. "Oh, look," one of them said, gesturing at Freddy. "It's my favorite science experiment."

The other one glanced at Billy. "You're new here," he said. "So you don't know the lay of the land. I'm Brett, and this is my brother Burke. We're scientists," he said, gesturing at the two of them.

"Yeah," Burke added, grinning meanly. "We study the

effects of violence on losers." He knocked the crutch out of Freddy's hand. Freddy reeled, almost falling.

"Hey!" he said angrily.

"Another data point for our project!" Burke said. The twins strutted off, laughing, and Freddy glared after them.

Billy frowned as well. *Keep a low profile*, he reminded himself. *Don't make waves, and get out of here as soon as you can.* His frown turned into a wince as Darla flung her arms around his waist in a tight hug.

"Have a good first day, big brother!" she said.

"Yeah," Billy said awkwardly. "About that. You can stop hugging me all the time. It's not like we're actually family. . . ." Darla's face crumpled, and her eyes filled with tears. Behind her, Freddy made a frantic *stop* signal with his hands.

"I mean, uh," Billy said, frantically backpedaling, but Pedro was pulling her away, slinging his arm comfortingly around her shoulders.

Great, Billy thought. *You made the unicorn cry.*

School was . . . school. Billy had been to five different schools in the last year, and they all kind of blended together. Reading *The Catcher in the Rye* for the third time in English class. Studying past tense in Spanish for the fourth time. Avoiding bullies and busybodies in the hallway for the eight hundred millionth time. He could do it in his sleep.

But avoiding Freddy . . . now, that was a new one.

"Flight or invisibility?" Freddy asked, plopping down next to Billy in the cafeteria. So much for lunch. Billy stood up from the empty table he'd parked himself at and made for the door. But Freddy followed him.

"Most people say flight," Freddy went on, apparently undaunted, "because heroes fly. Superman flies. And invisibility—that's creepy, right? That isn't a hero power. Even Batman doesn't have actual invisibility."

Billy kept walking. And Freddy hurried along beside him.

"But then they did a study," he said, "where you could answer anonymously. And you know what people said, when they knew nobody would know it was them?"

Billy didn't answer. He felt sorry for Freddy, but no way was he encouraging this. He didn't want siblings, and he didn't want friends, and he had a feeling Freddy was a magnet for trouble—which he *really* didn't want.

"They all chose invisibility!" Freddy said triumphantly. "Because most people—even good people—don't feel like a hero on the inside."

Billy was nearly at the cafeteria door.

"You're gonna run away," Freddy said, his voice suddenly serious. Billy froze, then turned around.

"You stole my Superman bullet," Freddy said, and Billy winced. He'd really thought Freddy hadn't noticed.

"I get it," Freddy said gently. "You don't trust anyone. But that's the thing about invisibility—you end up alone."

Billy looked away. That almost hurt. But he was used to being alone—being alone was kind of the point. He didn't need random people tying him down.

"I didn't steal your dumb bullet," Billy said unconvincingly as the buzzer sounded. Lunch was over—back to class.

Saved by the bell.

⚡⚡⚡

The group-home kids gathered in front of the school when the day was over, to walk home together. Billy joined them but made a point of staying out of their conversation. Mary might have screwed up his exit last night, but that didn't mean he wasn't still going to make a break for it the first chance he got.

". . . the teacher said I was in trouble for going over the fence at recess," Darla was telling Freddy. "But then I explained that I had to save that bee from drowning in a puddle, and she didn't even give me detention! Which is actually too bad? Because you meet the most fascinating people in detention! Oh well. Next time."

Whatever Freddy said in response was drowned out by an engine roaring as Brett and Burke tore past in a souped-up pickup truck. The truck swung so close to the kids that it clipped Freddy's crutch, wrenching it out of his hand . . . again. Billy rolled his eyes. These guys were grade-A jerks.

The truck stopped with a screech, and Brett and Burke piled out. Burke examined the bumper where it had hit the crutch. There was a very small scratch. Burke glowered.

Brett stalked toward Freddy, who was just getting his footing back, and knocked him to the ground.

"Hey!" Mary said, putting herself between Brett and Freddy. But Brett shoved her out of the way.

"Stop!" Darla yelled as Burke kicked Freddy in the stomach and Brett followed suit. Billy winced. Beside him, Pedro swallowed hard, then stepped forward like he was going to join the fight.

Brett grinned at Pedro and got in his face, looming over him. "What's up, porky?" he said, sneering. He balled up a fist and moved it until it was right under Pedro's chin. "You want some, too?"

Billy watched as sweat sprang up on Pedro's forehead. The poor guy looked terrified, but he wasn't backing down. It almost made Billy want to jump in himself.

Keep your head down, he reminded himself. He needed to get away from these people, not to get involved in their problems. He pulled his hoodie up over his head and began to walk away. *Just leave it. It isn't your business.*

Behind him, Brett and Burke continued to torment Freddy, playing keep-away with his crutch.

"What're you going to do?" Billy heard Burke ask Freddy. "Go crying to your mom?"

Billy stopped.

"Oh, right," Burke went on, "*you don't have a mom.*"

Billy turned around. Forget about keeping a low profile—this guy was just asking for it. He charged into the fray, grabbing Freddy's crutch from Brett and swinging it like a baseball bat.

Wham! It connected with Burke's body, and Burke

went down hard. Before anyone could react, Billy spun the crutch around and drove it into Brett's stomach. Then he thrust the crutch back into Freddy's hands and hightailed it. After some grunting and gasping, Brett and Burke got themselves together and scrambled after him.

Billy thought fast as he ran. The twins moved quicker than he did, so he'd have to lose them somehow—and fast.

The subway! Billy spotted a subway stop and made for it. He pounded down the stairs, and somebody up there must have been watching out for him, because a train was just pulling in. Billy put on a final desperate burst of speed and slid into the train car just as the doors were closing. Hot on his heels, Brett and Burke slammed into the closed doors, pounding at them fruitlessly as the train pulled out of the station.

Billy grinned wide, waving a cheerful goodbye.

As the train entered the dark subway tunnel, Billy slumped down into a seat, panting. He looked around him—he was the only person in the car. Good. The last thing he needed was some busybody asking him if he needed help. He tipped his head up and concentrated on getting his breath back. The train rocked gently as it sped through the tunnel.

And then it gave a great lurch and started moving faster . . . and faster. The lights flickered, and the electronic station map distorted into a series of weird symbols. Billy stood up, alarmed. What was happening?

With a loud screech, the train slammed to a stop. Billy was thrown to the dirty floor. When he scrambled up, the doors were opening . . . but they weren't in any subway station he'd ever seen before.

Beyond the open doors of the train lay an ancient stone temple.

CHAPTER 5

Billy's head spun from the unreality of it all as he stepped out of the subway car and into the dark, cavernous space. When he turned around, the subway car was gone.

"Great," Billy said to himself, his voice shaking. It vanished into the muffled silence of the temple. He looked around, his eyes adjusting to the gloom. Stone walls that looked like they'd been crumbling for centuries. Dust so thick you could use it as a blanket. The small, rough stone room opened onto a bridge that led across a chasm to a stone wall dotted with doors.

Carefully, Billy stepped onto the bridge. It shivered under his feet, and a great grinding noise filled the air as it rose and rotated through space.

"Oh god," Billy muttered, throwing his arms out and doing his best to stay very steady while the bridge spun through the air. Eventually, it slowed to a stop, lining up with a hoarse screech against one of the doors on the far side of the gap. Billy made his way carefully across the now-still bridge and through the door.

What *was* this place? Beyond the door he emerged into an echoing hall with pillars that stretched up as high as the eye could follow—the ceiling was nearly impossible to make out. There were signs of a recent fight: footsteps scuffed in the dust, and a row of objects in a broken case along one wall. A violin, sputtering with smokeless fire. A golden helmet. And a small glass box that looked like it had been home to some small creature, now empty and shattered.

"Hello?" Billy called, but no reply came except a distant echo. One side of the room was lined with piles of rubble and dust, shattered bits of sculpted stone sticking out from the piles here and there. Billy spotted a clawlike hand, half of a face, its mouth open in an evil grin, and a twisted, forked tail. And at the end of the room was a raised platform with seven thrones, all of them empty, except . . .

Billy froze, his heart pounding. The figure on the seventh throne was so still that he almost looked like a statue himself. But then he raised his head and fixed Billy with a sharp glare. The old man looked like he was half-alive at best—several wounds on his arm and shoulder were surrounded by a creeping black. He looked as though he was burning up from within.

"Hi," Billy said nervously. How long had he been sitting there? Who was he? What had *happened* in here?

"Uh," he started again, "I think I missed my subway stop."

"Billy Batson," the old man said. His voice rang like the world's rustiest bell.

Billy's blood ran cold. "Who's asking?" he said.

The old man heaved himself up out of the throne, moving as though every step was an agony. Guessing from his wounds, it probably was. Billy backed up a step.

"I am the last of the Council of Wizards," the Wizard said, his eyes never leaving Billy's. "The Keeper of the Rock of Eternity. Long ago, we chose a Champion."

"Uh," Billy said. "Okay?"

The Wizard sighed. "But we chose recklessly." He gestured with his staff, and a moving image sprang out of nowhere. Billy watched, transfixed, as a shadowy figure unleashed dark magic. Black lightning streamed from his fingers.

"And thus, the Seven Deadly Sins were released," the Wizard continued, as, within the hologram, seven twisted shadows streamed into being. "They spread chaos and injustice. They poisoned your kind."

Despite himself, Billy stepped closer, examining the projection—or whatever it was. "How are you doing this?" he asked. He couldn't see any sign of a projector or a screen—what kind of technology *was* this?

"I decided to never again share my magic—unless I could find one who was truly strong in spirit and pure of heart," the Wizard continued, looking at Billy expectantly.

Billy stared back at him. This guy was kidding himself. He was half willing to believe the "magic" thing—if Superman could be an alien from outer space, then maybe this guy could be an ancient magician. But as for the other part of it—Billy had been in the world long enough to know there was no such thing as "pure of heart."

"Look," he said, feeling kind of sorry for the old guy.

"Maybe this *is* magic"—he gestured to the hologram—"but 'pure of heart'? That's not me."

Disappointment swept over the Wizard's lined face.

"I think," Billy said as gently as he could, "you're looking for something that doesn't exist."

The Wizard slumped, and the image flickered and vanished. It was as though the last spark had burned out inside him.

"Perhaps it is as you say," the Wizard rasped. "But you are all I have. It is you—" He stumbled as his legs gave out, and Billy lunged forward to help him.

"—or nothing," the Wizard finished, leaning heavily on Billy. He looked up into Billy's eyes. "You must *find* the good in your heart. *Find* your will."

Billy shook his head, dazed. What was even happening? Why was he going along with this?

The Wizard held out his staff. "Put your hand on it," he said, "and say my name, and you will receive my power."

Traces of lightning crackled in his hair and lit up his eyes. "I choose you as Champion, Billy Batson."

"Look, this is nice of you and all . . . ," Billy started, trying to pull away. The Wizard's face darkened like a thundercloud.

"My family was struck down by the Sins! The thrones

stand empty!" he cried, lightning flashing in his eyes. Billy flinched. "Without a Champion, *nothing* can stop the Sins—the whole world will fall! *Do you understand?*"

Billy stared at him. "No," he admitted.

The Wizard glowered at him and pointed at the empty thrones. "*The seven Champions are mankind's only protection against the Sins*," he said in a voice you'd use to explain something very obvious to somebody very obnoxious. "I am the last of their number, and I am *dying*, child. Now *SPEAK MY NAME*."

Billy blinked. "Okay, don't freak out," he said, "but I don't *know* your name. We, like, just met."

The Wizard blinked, once, and the pressure in Billy's head eased up a bit. The Wizard nodded, grave. "My name," he said, "is Shazam."

All the tension bled out of Billy, and he snorted. *Shazam*, he thought. *Good one.* He'd almost bought it for a second. The whole *take my power, chosen one* thing. It was actually a pretty good joke when you thought about it. Shazam. The name was obviously too silly to be real.

But the Wizard wasn't laughing. He looked angrier than ever.

"Uh," Billy said incredulously, "are you serious?"

"*SAY IT!*" the Wizard roared, and Billy jumped a

mile. The Wizard thrust his staff out, and Billy grabbed it automatically.

"Okay," he said uncertainly, "so, just say it? Like, 'Shazam'?"

⚡⚡⚡

When Billy was nine years old, he'd been hit by a car. The car was very big, and Billy was very small, and he'd gone flying. One moment he was running across the parking lot, and the next he was hitting the ground several feet away. He'd never forgotten the feeling of the impact—it had felt like his soul was being wrenched from his body. He'd ended up with nothing worse than a broken arm and a few months of nightmares—waking in the dark, unable to forget how it had felt to be punched into the air by two tons of steel and rubber.

This was about a hundred times worse.

Raw power coursed through Billy's body. He felt all his nerves light up at once. He could feel his *spleen*, which he didn't like at all. Why did he even *have* a spleen in the first place? His teeth clenched so hard he thought they'd break, and the world went white as his eyeballs fizzed in their sockets.

And then it was over.

Billy stood up. (When had he fallen?) He shakily brushed the dust off his tight red pants, the gold gauntlets (gold gauntlets?) around his wrists catching the dim light in the Rock of Eternity.

"I feel really weird," he said, because he did. His deep voice (deep voice?!) echoed in the stone chamber.

Something was very, very, very wrong.

Billy looked at his hands. They were big and hairy. His feet were *huge*, and he was wearing golden boots. His broad, manly chest—*what?!*—had a huge, glowing lightning bolt on it.

Billy Batson was over six feet tall, and he was wearing a *cape*.

"It is done," the Wizard said. He coughed, a rattling, deathly sound. Billy looked at him, alarmed. The charred, black rot around his wounds had spread to cover nearly his entire body.

With visible effort, the Wizard drew one final breath. "Only you can unlock your true potential," he rasped. "Only you can restore the thrones—"

And with those words, he was gone, his body stiffening into a blackened statue and then crumbling to dust.

Horrified, Billy staggered back. He threw the staff to

the floor and looked around frantically. The walls felt like they were closing in on him. He was in the wrong body, in a forgotten tomb god knows where, and he wanted out.

Subway, subway, subway, he thought frantically. Where was the subway?

The world lurched and spun, and when his vision cleared, Billy was on a crowded subway car.

And every single person there was staring at him.

CHAPTER 6

"Uh," Billy said uncomfortably, his weird, deep voice booming, "hi."

Everyone stared at him for another moment before most of the people in the subway car visibly lost interest. Apparently, another random person in a cape didn't surprise anyone very much.

He hung on to the pole as the subway car swayed on its tracks, and caught his reflection in the dark window of the train. A completely new face stared back at him. Square jaw. Dark, slicked-back hair. And . . . yeah, that was one heck of a costume. The golden lightning bolt on his chest glowed steadily.

What the heck had *happened*? Was he stuck like this now? Did he have powers? Was he . . .

Was he a *super hero* now?

Billy's head spun. He couldn't just walk around like this. But he also couldn't show up back at the group home and just, like, sit down for dinner like nothing had happened. And he couldn't really run away, either—he'd never be able to blend into a crowd like this. He had to figure out what had happened, and what to do about it. He needed an expert. He needed someone . . .

Someone like Freddy. In fact, scratch that: he needed *Freddy*. Freddy was a super hero fanboy—he knew everything. Freddy would be able to help.

⚡⚡⚡

"Get back! I know kung fu!" Freddy yelped when Billy stuck his head in through the kitchen window at the group home. He'd snuck around the side of the house, peering into the windows as he went, until he found Freddy in the kitchen, washing dishes. Thankfully, he was alone.

"Seriously, I'll call the cops!" Freddy went on, fumbling

for his cell phone. Billy rolled his eyes. "Dude, it's *me*," he said.

Freddy looked up from where he was dialing 911. "That doesn't exactly clear things up," he said. But at least he'd stopped dialing.

"It's Billy," Billy said. "I need your help. Something really weird happened to me."

Freddy frowned. "Prove it," he said. Billy thought for a moment.

"You asked me if I'd choose flight or invisibility," he said. "I thought it was a dumb question, but right now I'd choose invisibility in a heartbeat, okay? And I *need your help*!"

Freddy's eyes widened. He grabbed for his crutch.

Thirty seconds later, Billy and Freddy were huddling in a shadow in the alley behind the house, and Freddy was plucking excitedly at Billy's cape.

"This is *amazing*!" he said. "Do you have powers? What kind of powers . . ." His eyes narrowed. "Wait a minute," he said suspiciously. "How do I know you aren't a telepathic super-villain putting a mind whammy on me to make me *believe* you're Billy?"

Billy fumbled for his backpack. He held his hand out.

The squashed Superman bullet lay on his palm in its little baggie.

"I lied," Billy admitted. "I stole your bullet."

Freddy stared at the baggie in Billy's hand. He looked disappointed, but not especially surprised. For the first time, Billy felt a pang of conscience.

"Uh," he added awkwardly, "sorry."

Freddy nodded shakily. "Yeah," he said, "that was a crappy thing to do."

Then he reached out and touched the lightning emblem on Billy's chest. Electricity crackled, and Freddy's hair stood on end.

"Geez," Freddy said, hushed. He looked up at Billy. "What *happened*, anyway?"

Billy took a deep breath and launched into the whole story. Freddy's eyes got wider and wider as Billy went on.

". . . and then suddenly I was on the subway," Billy finished, "in this big weird body, wearing *this*." He gestured at the skintight uniform. "And I figured you could help me figure things out."

Freddy frowned thoughtfully. "So what powers do you have?"

Billy shrugged helplessly. "How would I know? I don't

even know how to pee in this thing!"

Freddy's eyes widened. "Do you think you can *fly*?" he asked.

Billy grinned. "Won't know if I don't try," he said.

"Ow," Billy said. He peeled himself off the street, wincing.

"That's a no on flight," Freddy said thoughtfully.

"No kidding," Billy said. Even in a super hero's body, falling six feet onto the pavement after jumping out of a tree, well, it still stung.

Freddy helped him up.

"Let's try invisibility next," he suggested. Billy nodded. That sounded less painful. He closed his eyes and concentrated. *Invisible, invisible, I'm invisible,* he chanted in his mind. He pictured himself fading from sight. His brightly costumed body going transparent, then . . . vanishing altogether.

Cautiously, Billy opened his eyes. Freddy stood in front of him, looking around the busy Philadelphia street wildly. "Billy?" he called. "Billy, are you there? Where did you go?"

"You can't see me?!" Billy said, his heart hammering in his chest. He was invisible! It had worked!

"Where are you?" Freddy said, turning in the wrong direction entirely.

"I'm right here!" Billy said, laughing. He waved his arms wildly and jumped up and down. He was invisible! Nobody could see him!

"Cute cape, weirdo," said a teenaged girl as she walked by with a group of friends. They all snickered. Billy froze, mortified. Freddy turned around, laughing.

"That's a no on invisibility," he said, "and a no on super-intelligence."

Billy pointed an angry finger. "So help me," he said, "I'm gonna kick your—"

A spark of electricity shot out of Billy's finger. He stared in shock as it flew straight at Freddy, who ducked just in time. The lightning hit a power pole instead, and the wires crackled. Then, *BOOM!* All the lights in the neighborhood went out. The world plunged into darkness.

Freddy and Billy stared at each other in the moonlight. A chorus of angry yells came from all the houses around them, but Billy didn't care. He knew what his power was. And it was awesome.

Freddy pointed at the lightning bolt still glowing on Billy's chest.

"The answer was there all along!" he said.

CHAPTER 7

"Where are we going?" Billy asked, bewildered, as Freddy tugged him along. He was twice Freddy's size now, but Freddy just pulled him along as if he were a toddler. He had one hand fisted in Billy's cape, and an official-looking clipboard tucked under his arm.

"To try out your lightning powers somewhere safer," Freddy said. "I don't want you frying an old lady or a cat or something by accident."

They turned a corner and Freddy pointed triumphantly. "There!" he said.

Billy squinted. "A playground?" he asked doubtfully. The park was full of metal jungle gyms.

"Light 'em up!" Freddy said cheerfully.

Billy stared at him, a grin growing wider and wider on his face.

"Oh yeah," he said. This was going to be fun.

Billy straightened up and pointed his finger at a nearby play dome. He reached inside himself for the same source of power he'd felt when he nearly zapped Freddy by accident. It was there—a bottomless vault of electricity, just waiting to be discharged. He took a deep breath and let it out.

BLAM.

Lightning split the air with a deafening peal and arced from Billy's hand to the jungle gym. It traced around the bars of the structure, lighting up the entire playground. It looked like something from a movie.

Beside him, Freddy yelled. "Oh yeah!"

Billy turned to him, sparks and traces of lightning still clinging to his hand, and held it up for a high five. Freddy slammed his palm against Billy's. The last of the lightning harmlessly sparked across Freddy's fingers when he pulled his hand away, and he watched it, fascinated.

"We gotta come up with a super hero name for you,"

Freddy said. "Something to do with lightning, maybe."

"Yeah—" Billy started, but he was interrupted by a shrill scream.

"HELP!" a frantic cry came from the alleyway halfway down the block. Billy and Freddy both whipped around. It sounded like someone was getting mugged. Billy had lived in enough rough neighborhoods to know to stay far away from that kind of situation. You didn't want to get involved.

He started to turn away, but Freddy wasn't following him. Billy looked back and found Freddy standing in place, staring expectantly at Billy.

"What?" Billy said. Freddy looked him up and down and raised an eyebrow.

"Oh, right," Billy said. He was a super hero now. He kind of *had* to get involved. And fast, before things got worse in that alley.

He took off running—

—and a split second later, he was barreling into the mugger.

The mugger hit the pavement hard. Billy shook his head, confused. He looked back at Freddy . . . who was still standing a hundred yards away. Freddy waved cheerfully and raised his clipboard.

"Hyper-speed!" he yelled. "Check!" He ticked something off on the clipboard. Billy rolled his eyes and turned back to the crime scene. The mugger was trying to pick himself up off the ground. The lady he'd been mugging yanked her purse out of his hand and kicked him hard. He went back down again.

"That'll teach you to mug old ladies," Billy said.

"I'm forty," the woman said indignantly. "I'm the same age as you."

"Oh, right," Billy said. "I am definitely forty years old! Or at least I'm somewhere in that range. You know, adult range. Absolutely. I'm an adult."

The woman squinted at him suspiciously. "I'm sorry," she said, "who are you?"

"Thundercrack!" Freddy said, hurrying up to them. "At last, a hero for Philadelphia! He's got the power—and speed!—of lightning!"

"Thundercrack sounds like the noise a fart makes," Billy said. On the ground, the mugger giggled. The woman kicked him again. "Ouch," he said.

Freddy thought it over. "Mister Philadelphia!" he suggested.

"That sounds like cream cheese," Billy said.

"Power Boy!" Freddy tried.

"No," Billy said flatly. "You're not calling me Power Boy."

"Power Boy," the woman said, "do you know this child?" She pointed at Freddy.

"He's my manager," Billy said. "And *please* don't call me that."

"I'm your manager?" Freddy said, so excited that his voice cracked. "I mean, uh, yes, ma'am. I'm his manager."

"Whatever," the mugger said, finally climbing to his feet. "You people are all crazy, and I'm out of here."

He started to run away, but Billy zipped in front of his path, using his super-speed to cut him off. "Now, you wait just a minute," he said, doing his best Superman impression. "I'm not done with you." He gave the guy a gentle shove to make his point, but the mugger sailed into the air and landed thirty feet down the alley with an *oof.* After a stunned moment, he scrambled up and ran away.

Billy stood still, too shocked to run after him. Had *he* done that?

Freddy whipped out his clipboard. "Super-strength," he said, jotting notes. He looked pumped.

"Look," said the woman, her voice shaking. "I don't know what's going on here, but I would like to just leave quietly, okay?" Billy turned to her, and saw that she was backing away slowly, rummaging around in her purse. He stepped toward her, his hands raised reassuringly. Lightning sparkled on his fingertips.

"Don't touch me!" the woman said. She looked deathly afraid . . . of him. Nobody had ever looked at Billy that way before, and he didn't like it. "I don't know who you are or what you want, but I don't want to end up airborne like that guy did just now. I have five cats who depend on me."

She took a wad of cash out of her wallet and thrust it into Billy's hands. "Here's all my money," she said. "Just let me leave, okay?"

Billy's hands automatically closed around the stack of bills. "Wait!" he said. "I'm not doing this for—"

But she had run out of the alley.

"Thanks for the donation!" Freddy called after her.

Billy stared down at the money in his hands. It was a *lot* of money.

It was *seventy-three dollars.*

"We're rich!" Billy said. He high-fived Freddy so hard he sent him sprawling. "Oh, dude, I'm sorry," he said.

"Whatever," Freddy said, climbing to his feet. "Come on, let's make it rain!"

The convenience store clerk's face lit up when Billy and Freddy walked in. "Superman!" she said. Then she got a better look at Billy's uniform. Her face fell. "Oh, she said. "I thought you were Superman. But you're just some guy."

"Hey," Billy said, offended, "I am way cooler than Superman. Can Superman do *this*?" He gestured at a counter display of candy bars, and lighting flew from his fingers. The candy bars exploded.

Covered in chocolate and bits of cellophane, the cashier stared at him coldly.

"Superman *wouldn't* do that," she said.

"I'll, uh, I can pay for that," Billy said.

"Power Boy is rich," Freddy explained.

The door dinged behind him, and two guys in stocking masks barged into the convenience store. "Everything out of the cash register and into this bag!" one of them yelled, while the other guy waved a big gun around.

Billy was already hiding under a display of Christmas decorations when he remembered who he was now. He stood up, tinsel flying in every direction, and said, "Halt!"

The thieves stopped and stared at him.

"Halt?" Freddy said. "Who says 'halt' anymore?"

"I dunno," Billy said. "It seemed like a super hero-y thing to say."

"Well, it didn't work," the guy with the big gun said. He pointed the gun at Billy and pulled the trigger.

It felt like time was suddenly moving very slowly. Billy could almost see the path of the bullet as it rocketed straight toward his chest. He was too shocked to use his super-speed to even try to dodge it. He just stood there and thought,

No—

But there was no impact, no pain, no blood. Instead there was a *plink*.

The bullet rebounded harmlessly off Billy's chest and bounced on the tiled floor.

"Shoot," the robber said, staring.

"You know," Billy said, a grin creeping over his face, "you tried that already. Didn't work great."

Freddy waved his clipboard so hard he nearly toppled over. "Bullet immunity!"

"What does that even mean?" Billy said. Freddy knew more long words than anyone he'd ever met.

"Dude, you're freaking bulletproof!" Freddy shrieked by way of explanation. He was scribbling fast.

"Oh," Billy said, "yeah, I kind of figured that part out." He reached out and plucked the gun from the robber's hand and bent the barrel like it was a bendy straw.

Being a super hero was *awesome.*

At that point it was all over but the crying, as one of Billy's foster moms used to like to say. He had the robbers tied up in Christmas lights before they could blink.

The cashier wouldn't even let him pay for the candy bars he'd destroyed. "On the house," she said, not cracking a smile. "You're still no Superman, but you're okay in my book, Power Boy. Now, did you want to actually buy something?"

"My name's not—" Billy started, but Freddy interrupted him.

"How much slushie can we get for seventy-three dollars?" he asked.

The answer, as it turned out, was: a *lot* of slushie.

CHAPTER 8

Billy's new body was great for lots of things, but sneaking wasn't one of them. It also didn't help that he had a stomachache after drinking about thirty slushies. He had the worst sugar headache of his entire life, and his tongue was probably stained blue permanently. He didn't need to see it in a mirror to know that. It *felt* blue.

"Shhhh," Freddy hissed at him as Billy tripped over a footstool in the dark living room of the group home.

"Sorry," Billy whispered. He couldn't figure out how Freddy was managing to be so quiet. After all, he'd had the other half of the slushies, and he wasn't even a super hero.

Squeak! went the floorboard at the base of the stairs as Billy stepped on it.

"Dude!" Freddy whispered.

"Sorry!" Billy said again.

"Why are we even here?" Billy whispered as they climbed the stairs. "I can't stay here looking like this!"

"Yeah," Freddy agreed, looking back at him. "You're definitely going to need a lair or something. But we'll have to make this work for tonight."

Suddenly, Freddy froze on the stairs. He held a hand up. Below them, the front hall brightened as the kitchen light went on. Billy could hear Victor and Rosa in the kitchen.

"The kids said he ran off after school," Rosa said. Her voice sounded tired and sad. "We couldn't even keep him here two days."

"You and I both ran away at least a couple of times back in our foster kid days," Victor said. "Even Mary's run off once or twice."

Rosa sighed. "This could have been *home* for him," she said. Something in Billy's heart twanged painfully.

"Baby, do you remember what you told me the second time Mary ran away?" Victor asked. "You said, 'Home isn't something you're given, it's something you choose.' He has to choose."

Ahead of Billy, Freddy started back up the stairway. Billy followed him, but his heart was still beating fast in his chest. Something about the way Rosa had sounded. Something about what Victor had said. It was hard not to care—hard not to wish things could be different.

Billy was so distracted thinking about it that he tripped over his own feet, slamming his knee loudly (and painfully) into one of the steps.

"Mmmph!" He tried to smother his own yelp, but he still made way more noise than he meant to.

There was a startled silence from the kitchen. Ahead of Billy, Freddy put his face into his palm and shook his head.

"Who's there?" Rosa called.

"Uh," Freddy said, aiming for casual and missing by a mile, "it's just me! Freddy! Just Freddy. All by himself. Myself. Going to bed. In my room. All by myself."

"Weak," Billy whispered. "Super weak."

"Shut! Up!" Freddy hissed.

"Good night, Freddy," Victor called up. "Try to get some rest."

"Night," Freddy called.

"Night," Billy said automatically, his deep adult voice

booming. *Oh, crap.* He clapped both hands over his mouth, but it was too late.

Freddy stared at him incredulously. "Are you kidding me right now?!" he whisper-shouted at Billy. Billy stared at him mutely, his hands still over his mouth.

There was another silence from the kitchen. Then the sound of chairs scraping across the tiled floor as Rosa jumped up from the kitchen table.

"Who was that?" Rosa called up, her voice full of suspicion and alarm. Her steps were coming through the kitchen and approaching the front hall at the base of the stairs.

Billy and Freddy stared at each other in a panic.

"Uh," Freddy called down, "just Billy. He's back and he's *super tired*, which is why he sounds like that, and we're going to bed *right now*. Good night!" He waved his hand frantically at Billy. They scrambled up the stairs.

"Wait! Billy! Are you okay?" Rosa called.

"Super-*duper* tired! See you in the morning!" Freddy yelled as they reached the second-floor hallway. They could hear Rosa coming up the stairs. There was no time—no way they'd make it to Freddy's room. Billy opened the first door they came to, yanking Freddy in behind him and slamming it shut.

He turned around, heart hammering, and there, in the darkened room, was Darla. She was sitting up in bed, staring at them, her eyes wide with fear. In the other bed, Mary slept soundly, earplugs in and eye mask on.

"Billy? Freddy?" Rosa called from the hallway. They heard her footsteps pass Darla and Mary's door and head farther back toward Freddy's room.

Darla opened her mouth to scream, and Billy supersped his way across the room to cover her mouth with his giant hand.

"Darla!" he whispered urgently. "It's me! Billy! Don't be scared! I know I look weird, but I swear it's me. This Wizard made me into a super hero! He used his magic to slurp me into his weird old temple, and he gave me all of his power by having me say 'Shazam'—"

The moment he said the name, lightning engulfed Billy. The entire house felt like it was inside one big thunderclap, and blinding flashes of electricity sprang from every wall socket and the ceiling light fixture. Billy's whole body went rigid from the energy coursing through it, and when it was over, he felt weirdly light and wobbly.

Oh.

He felt light because he *was* lighter: he was back in his normal body.

Billy shook his head. What had happened? He'd said the name—that must be the trigger!

"Rosa!" Victor called from downstairs. Billy glanced out the window. The lights in the entire neighborhood were out again—because of him, again.

"Coming!" Rosa answered, and they heard her footsteps hurry down the hall and down the stairs.

Freddy laughed excitedly. He bonked Billy on the head with his clipboard and then immediately started scribbling as fast as he was talking. "You, my friend, have the power of verbally controlled physiological transformation!"

Billy and Darla looked at each other, then at Freddy.

"What?" they said in unison.

"You can switch!" Freddy crowed. "All you have to do is say—well, you know, say *that word*—and you can switch!"

Half-awakened by the lightning, Mary grumbled in her sleep and began to toss and turn. Billy and Freddy snuck back out into the darkened hallway, and Darla slipped through the door before they could close it, following them in her nightie and slippers. Downstairs, they could hear Rosa and Victor doing battle with the fuse box.

Darla stared at Billy, her eyes even huger.

"You're a—" she started, but Freddy cut her off.

"Nobody can know, Darla," he said firmly.

"Why?" Darla asked. "He's a super hero! They should put him on TV!"

"Nobody can know that he's really Billy Batson," Freddy said. "For him, but also for us. If people know who he is, then his loved ones could be in danger from supervillains."

Billy snorted. Freddy and Darla were both nice enough, but they hardly counted as "loved ones." He'd just met them two days ago!

Freddy glared at him. "Darla," he said, turning back to the little girl, "you can't tell *anyone*."

"But . . . ," Darla said, pouting.

"Darla," Billy said, staring deep into her eyes and giving her his best puppy-dog expression, "good sisters keep secrets."

Darla's eyes went even wider, and a blinding smile lit up her face. She threw her arms around Billy's waist.

"I won't let you down, big brother," she said. Billy awkwardly patted her head, feeling like a complete tool.

CHAPTER 9

The three-story mansion in Potomac, Maryland, was lit up brightly in the snowy night. Fluffy snowflakes floated down from the sky. They caught the warm light from the glowing windows of the house before they settled on the perfectly pruned shrubbery and the long line of expensive cars parked out front. Muffled Christmas music drifted out of the house and echoed through the cold night air. Inside the house, figures in fancy clothes could be glimpsed through the windows, drinking champagne and laughing.

The Sivana family's annual Christmas party was in full swing.

And then in the iron gray sky, a lone figure appeared, floating eerily against the dark clouds. After decades of bitter absence, with the Eye of Sin burning in his skull, Thaddeus Sivana was coming home.

Sivana drifted down silently from the cold night sky, power coursing through his veins. With the Sins inside him, he had nearly every power he'd ever dreamed of. And he was never alone: their hissing voices murmured at him every moment of every day.

Soon, hissed Pride. *Soon they'll see what you've become.*

You'll make them regret their abuses, Wrath chimed in.

You'll get what you are owed—, began Envy.

—and take what you deserve, finished Greed.

Sivana's feet touched the ground at the doorstep. He reached into his breast pocket and pulled out a pair of sunglasses. Sliding them on, he opened the door.

Inside, guests in holiday finery milled around, swilling champagne and gulping down hors d'oeuvres. Waiters dressed as Santa and his elves swept through the crowd with silver trays. A huge ice sculpture in the shape of the Sivana Industries logo dripped slowly. And Thaddeus Sivana's father, now nearly eighty years old, looked up from his chair and went pale with fury.

"What are you doing here?" Sivana's father demanded,

his voice high and quavering. The room went silent as everyone turned and stared at Sivana. Their faces showed disdain and disapproval. Sivana grinned. These people had no idea what was about to happen to them.

Make them suffer, Wrath whispered.

Make them see your true power, Pride whispered.

Ooh! Snacks! said Gluttony.

Sivana reached out and grabbed a handful of mini-quiches from a tray held by a waiter wearing reindeer horns and a bright red nose. He popped one into his mouth.

"Thad," said his brother Sid, now fifty and red-faced. He scowled. "This is a company event."

"Weird," Sivana said, chewing loudly. "Nobody invited me. But, hey, I wasn't offended. See, father," he added, grinning at the old man, "I've toughened up."

"You'll always be a disappointment," his father snapped.

"Please, Thaddeus," his mother said, smiling weakly. "You're embarrassing us in front of our guests."

"I'm here in the spirit of giving," Sivana explained. He yanked off his sunglasses. The Eye of Sin burned and twirled in his eye socket. The guests nearest him screamed and recoiled.

"Giving you all what you deserve," Sivana finished.

Black lightning crackled out from his fingers, and the screaming began in earnest.

⚡⚡⚡

The snow kept falling from the night sky, but now it was joined by the white flecks of ash and glowing embers that were swirling in the chill air. In the smoldering wreckage of the Sivana mansion, a lone figure sat at the charred remains of a grand dining room table.

"You always said I was a weakling," Sivana said. His father was dead and gone, along with everyone else who'd been in the house, but it still felt good to have the last word. "Look at me now. I'm the last with our name. I beat you. And I've got more power than your money and influence could ever get you. More power than *anyone*."

No, hissed Envy, writhing inside the Eye of Sin. *There is one who has more.*

Sivana stiffened. He knew who the Sin must be talking about.

"The Wizard," he said.

Destroy the Wizard . . . , hissed Sloth,

And all the magic . . . , said Lust,

In all the realms . . . , continued Gluttony,

Will be yours, finished Envy.

Sivana stood up. He knew what he had to do.

The elevator was blackened with soot, but it still stood in the center of the house. Sivana touched the "down" button and watched with satisfaction as power flowed from his finger, illuminating the frame around the door and lighting up seven familiar symbols. The doors slid open, and the dark and echoing halls of the Rock of Eternity appeared on the other side.

Smiling in satisfaction, Sivana stepped forward, his footsteps echoing in the ancient chamber.

"Show yourself, you old fool!" he called into the throne room as he entered.

But the seventh throne was empty, and his words bounced unanswered through the cavernous space.

A breeze swept a pile of ash into a little whirlwind and then dissipated. Sivana stared down at the ash.

The Wizard was already dead.

Curse him! cried Wrath.

The old man has appointed a Champion, added Greed.

You must find the Champion . . . , said Pride,

. . . and destroy him, said Wrath.

Take his magic, said Envy, *and you will finally be the strongest.*

Meet Billy Batson.

Billy Batson is fourteen, sharp, and streetwise as they come, and he knows how to take care of himself.

After Billy runs away from yet another foster home, he is placed with the Vasquez family. Victor and Rosa Vasquez have a noisy, cozy home.

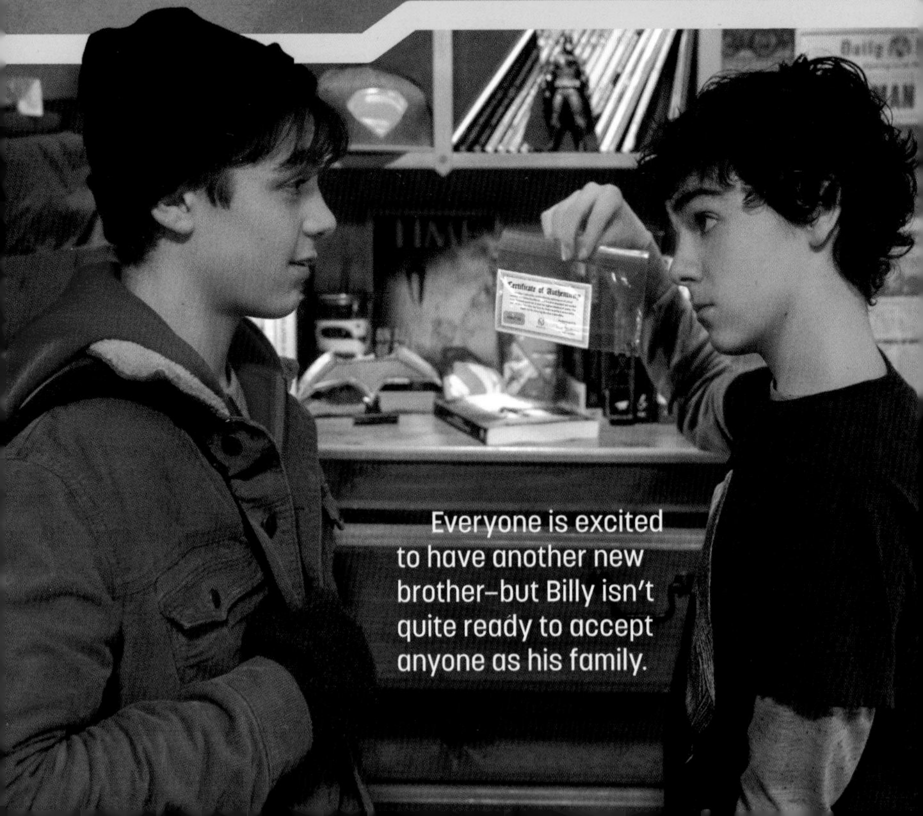

Everyone is excited to have another new brother—but Billy isn't quite ready to accept anyone as his family.

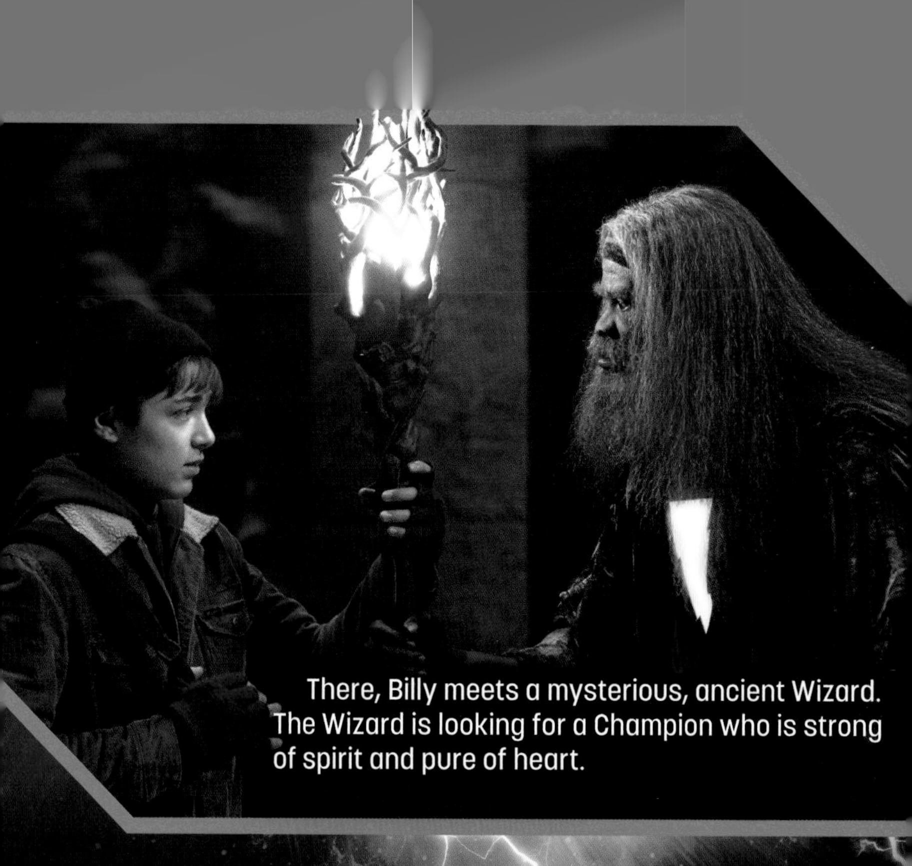

There, Billy meets a mysterious, ancient Wizard. The Wizard is looking for a Champion who is strong of spirit and pure of heart.

"I CHOOSE YOU AS CHAMPION, BILLY BATSON."

With just one word, Billy Batson is transformed. What's that one magic word?

SHAZAM!

What Billy doesn't know is that a dangerous enemy is not far away.

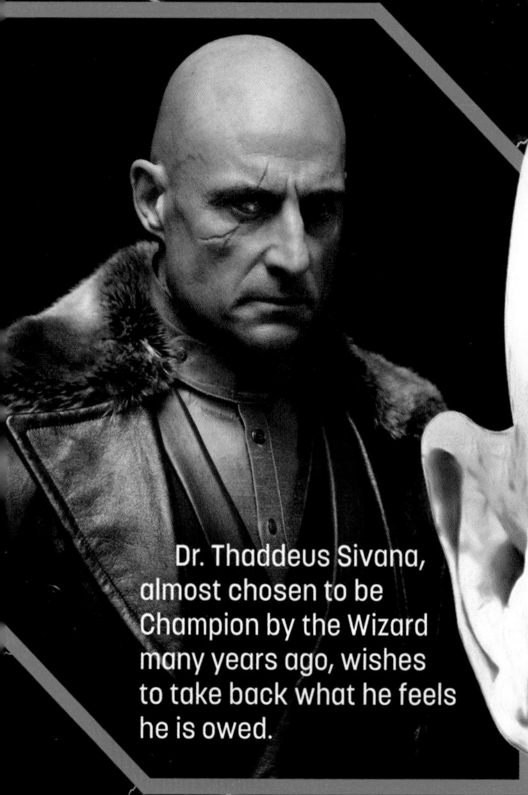

Dr. Thaddeus Sivana, almost chosen to be Champion by the Wizard many years ago, wishes to take back what he feels he is owed.

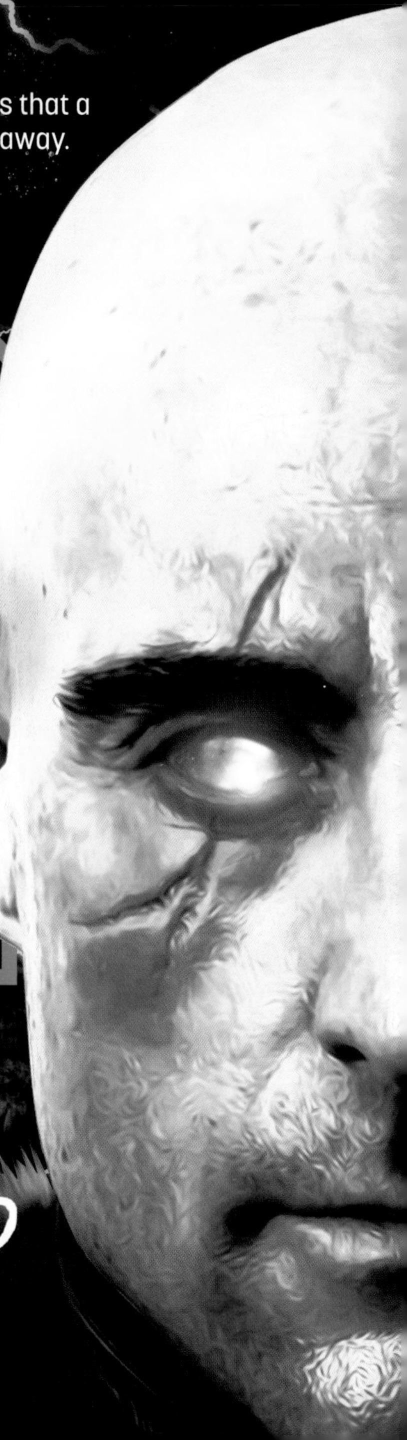

"I DON'T NEED TO E GOOD. I JUST NEED TO BE POWERFUL."

BEING A SUPER HERO HAS ITS PERKS.

Billy lets his foster brother Freddy in on his secret. Freddy just has one question: "So, what powers do you have?"

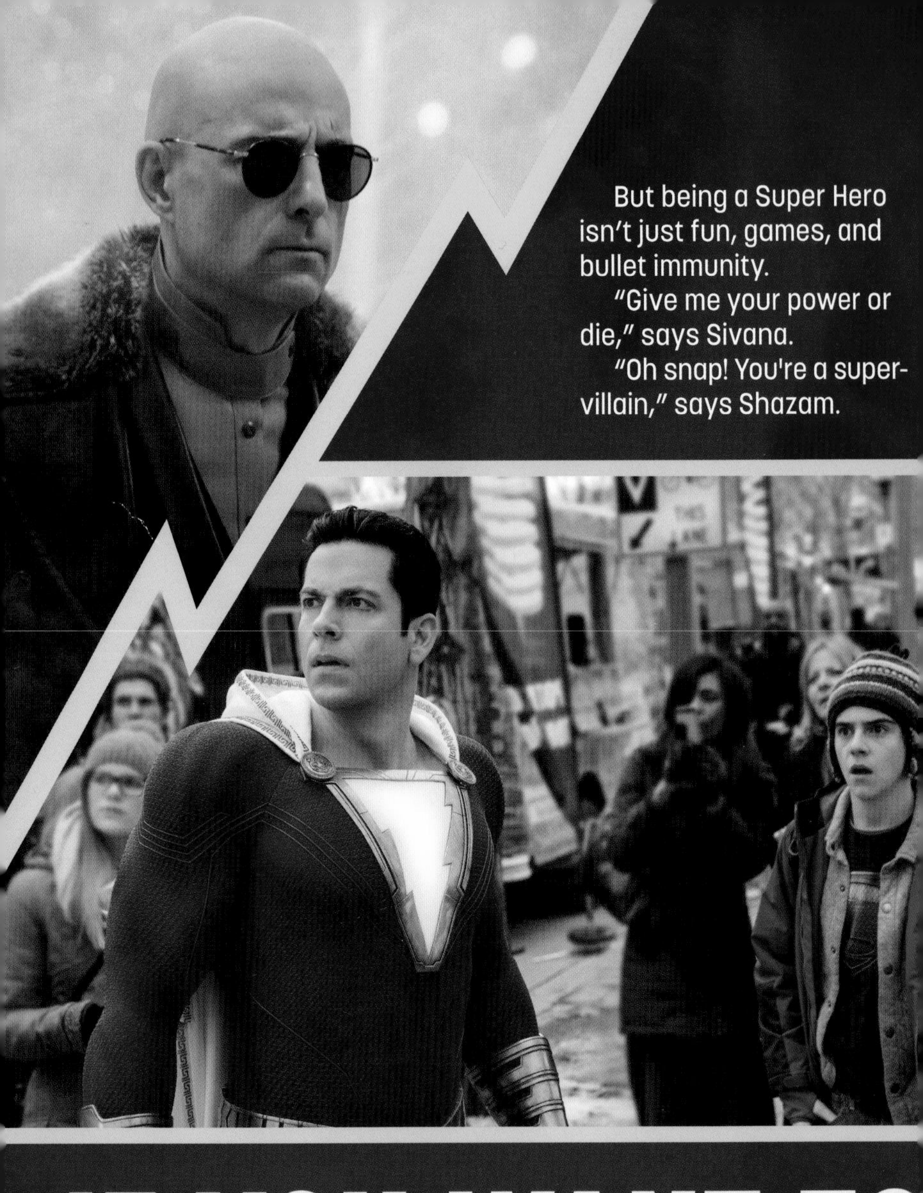

But being a Super Hero isn't just fun, games, and bullet immunity.

"Give me your power or die," says Sivana.

"Oh snap! You're a super-villain," says Shazam.

IF YOU WANT TO SAVE THE WORLD, JUST SAY THE MAGIC WORD.

CHAPTER 10

The lovingly polished pickup truck that pulled into the parking lot in front of Fawcett Central School had a small scratch on its front bumper. Billy noticed that Freddy winced when he saw it—he was still nursing bruises from the fight with Brett and Burke the other day.

The twins swaggered out of their truck, sneering at Freddy as he passed by.

"Nerd," one of them spat at Freddy.

"Freak," the other said.

Freddy ignored them, but Billy had had enough.

⚡⚡⚡

The very same lovingly polished pickup truck fell from the sky a few minutes later and landed with a deafening crash, a shattering bounce, and finally a sort of a grinding moan. . . . Well, *that* pickup truck had an awful lot more than just a scratch on its bumper.

Behind the school, Billy *Shazam*ed back into his normal body and strolled around the corner of the building just in time to see Brett and Burke's faces as they stared at the pile of crushed metal that used to be their truck.

Not looking up from his phone, which he was using to film every precious moment, Freddy raised his hand. Billy high-fived it, whistling innocently as the twins frantically looked for someone to blame.

The fun continued after school. Freddy was taking his role as Billy's manager seriously and had decided it was his job to 1) figure out all of Billy's powers, and 2) document them for the internet and make Billy's superpowered alter ego a viral sensation.

"What is this place?" Billy asked as Freddy led him up to a huge abandoned warehouse.

"Behold . . . ," Freddy said, gesturing at the heap of broken windows and crumbling concrete, ". . . your lair!"

Billy grinned. It was *perfect*.

"*Shazam!*" he said. Lightning arced around him as he grew into his big super hero form. Billy was starting to think of it as his "Shazam body."

They tackled the lightning first. With Freddy filming on his smartphone, Billy zapped target after target, including some airborne ones.

"Fore!" Freddy yelled, heaving his civics textbook into the air. Billy squinted and aimed both hands at the book, following it as it sailed across the yard behind the warehouse.

Boom, he thought, and lightning arced out from his hands, catching the book midair. It exploded, sending thousands of charred bits of paper fluttering through the air.

They messed around with Billy's lightning powers for a while, and then Freddy clapped his hands briskly and said, "Time to test your super-strength!"

They started small, with Billy lifting bigger and bigger piles of bricks. Then they moved on to a car someone had abandoned behind the warehouse. Billy got that into the air without much trouble.

Freddy looked around. "I'm kind of running out of heavy stuff for you," he said. Then he laughed. "Maybe you should just try lifting the entire warehouse!"

Billy shrugged. "I'll give it a shot," he said.

"Dude, I was joking!" Freddy yelped, but Billy was already squatting down by the corner of the foundation. He wormed his fingers under the concrete and started lifting. Nothing happened.

"Okay," Freddy said, still filming with his phone. "So the limit of your strength is somewhere in between a car and . . . a four-story industrial building the size of a city block. That doesn't really narrow it down much. . . ."

But Billy wasn't done. He took a deep breath and gripped hard with both hands wedged under the corner of the building. *Come on*, he thought. *I bet you can do this.* His muscles bunched and strained, and his feet dug into the pavement so hard it started to crack under his boots.

Bit by bit, the foundation rose up. Half an inch, then an inch, then several inches. Then several feet. Sweating and panting, Billy heaved himself to his feet, still gripping the corner of the foundation. The entire building started creaking and shivering. Windows shattered and glass rained down on him. The concrete walls began to groan alarmingly.

"Stop!" Freddy yelled. "Stop, it's gonna break up!"

Very carefully, Billy lowered the foundation back into place. The building gave a sort of sigh as it settled back down. Billy patted it reassuringly, then flopped down on his back. His heart was racing and his arms felt like noodles, but he'd *done* it.

He looked up to see Freddy's smartphone pointing straight down at him.

"That was kinda hard," Billy said breathlessly.

"Dude," Freddy said. "You just power-lifted a freaking warehouse. This is going on the internet *right now.*"

⚡⚡⚡

By five p.m., the social media accounts Freddy had set up for Philadelphia's new favorite super hero (Freddy named them all HeroManager, naturally) had over a million followers each. Freddy kept staring at his phone.

"You're getting an average of seventeen thousand likes per second," Freddy said, his voice hushed as he checked the account again. They were walking down a busy Philadelphia street, Billy strutting in his gold boots with his cape fluttering. Freddy kept walking into telephone poles. He couldn't stop checking his social accounts.

Billy nodded cheerfully. He was awesome, and now the world knew it. He zapped some lightning into the smartphone a passerby was holding.

"Charged your phone," he said jauntily. He pointed at another person's phone. "And your phone"—and another—

"and your phone"—and another. This was *fun*. How come you never saw other super heroes out having fun? Billy snorted. Because they were boring, and he was *not boring*.

"Aaaaand," he said, zapping another person's phone, "charged *your* phone." He put a little more juice into it than he'd meant to, and the phone caught on fire and sort of exploded. The guy dropped it and yelped, "Hey, what the heck?"

"Everyone at the office will love this story," Billy shot back over his shoulder, winking at the guy. "You're welcome!"

The guy just shook his fist.

Some people just didn't know the meaning of gratitude.

⚡⚡⚡

Nobody got *anything* done at school the next day. During break, the halls were packed with kids watching videos of Philadelphia's mysterious new super hero on their phones. During class, none of the students could concentrate on anything. Even the teachers were talking about the mystery hero.

Billy walked through the school, eating it up. This was the best secret ever.

"I think he's *so cute*," a pretty girl was telling her friends as Billy and Freddy walked by.

"Those muscles!" one of them said.

"That jawline!" said another.

They all sighed loudly. Billy walked a little straighter, a big grin on his face.

"You know," Freddy said loudly, "I bet the guy taking those videos is awesome. It's actually really brave of him. I think maybe *he's* the real hero."

He was so worked up that he walked right into Burke.

"Oof!" Freddy bounced back and staggered a couple of steps before regaining his balance.

"Watch it, peg leg," Burke said, sneering at Freddy.

"That doesn't even make any sense," Freddy said. "I mean, you could have called me 'three legs' or 'tripod' or something, but 'peg leg' implies I have a prosthetic leg, which I obviously don't." He gestured at his flesh-and-bone ankles. "Do me a favor and try to make fun of me correctly, okay?"

"Cool," Brett said. "Now we have another reason to beat you up: you're clumsy *and* annoying." He raised a fist, but Freddy threw up a hand.

"I wouldn't do that if I were you!" he said in a rush.

"You're really gonna regret it."

Brett laughed. "I never have before," he said. He raised his fist again.

"No," Freddy said, glancing at Billy, "I mean it. I have this friend, see—"

Billy's heart sank. Suddenly, he saw where this was going.

"*Freddy*," he hissed, poking his friend in the side discreetly. But there was no stopping him.

"You touch a hair on my head," Freddy said, getting in Brett's face, "and my friend will hunt you down and *destroy* you. You might have heard of him. He's, uh, a man of many names. On the internet. They call him the Human Power Strip. Zap-tain America. The Electrician. Power Boy—"

"They *do not* call him Power Boy!" Billy protested.

"—Sir Zaps-A-Lot. The Lightning Bug. Incandescent Man. The Cape. Power Boy."

"*Dude!*" Billy said, elbowing Freddy again.

"Right," Burke said scornfully. "*You* know Power Boy."

"We're really close," Freddy said defiantly. "Literally. Really close."

Billy stomped on his foot.

"Ow!" Freddy said.

"Prove it," said Brett, "and maybe we let you live."

"I *can* prove it," Freddy said, a little desperately. "He's coming here tomorrow. He's, uh, he's gonna have lunch with me. In the cafeteria."

Crap, Billy thought. He put his hand over his eyes.

"Whatever, loser," Brett said as the class bell rang. "You're pathetic."

"You'll see!" Freddy insisted. "He'll be here!"

"And when he's not," Burke said, "we will be." He pounded a fist into his open palm as he turned and walked away.

CHAPTER 11

"What the heck were you thinking?" Billy whisper-yelled, as soon as they were alone in the hall. "*You* were the one who said we had to be super careful about my secret identity, and now you want me showing up as him *at my own school*?"

"It's not a big deal!" Freddy said. "I don't get what the problem is."

"The problem," Billy said coldly, "is you're *using* me." He turned and started walking away. He was late to class already.

"But Billy," Freddy said, and something in his tone

made Billy stop. "They're gonna beat me up. Again. I don't know how much more of this I can take."

This isn't your problem, Billy reminded himself. He didn't owe Freddy anything. Freddy and Darla and the rest of them might like to pretend that Billy was somehow now part of their family just because he'd been placed in the same group home as them. But he wasn't. It was time Freddy realized that.

Without a word, Billy walked down the hall and turned the corner, leaving Freddy alone.

"Okay," Freddy called after him, his voice quavering. "So you-know-who will be there at lunch tomorrow. Right?"

⚡⚡⚡

Billy didn't even bother going into the school the next day. He'd taken one look at the line for the metal detector and thought, *Why am I still doing this?*

He didn't have to spend his day as a teenager in a prison pretending to be a school. He could spend his day as a super hero celebrity having fun with his awesome powers. It was a no-brainer.

So he turned on his heel and walked in the general direction of downtown. Once he was far enough from school that nobody would recognize him, he snuck behind a garbage truck and waited until nobody was watching. And then . . .

Shazam!

Lightning coursed through his body, and when his vision cleared, Billy was a super hero again. He stepped out from behind the garbage truck and struck a heroic pose on the busy sidewalk. Within minutes, he was in the center of a crowd of admirers. They were all fighting to get closer to him—trying to get his attention. Billy grinned. This was *way* more fun than civics class.

"Red Cyclone!" someone yelled. "Can I take a picture with you?"

"Mister Cape!" someone else called, "please can you sign my cast?"

Billy thought fast. If he handled this right, he could make a *lot* of money, really fast.

"Ten dollars for photos!" he announced to the crowd, "and fifteen for autographs." People started fumbling for their wallets, and Billy grinned. *Jackpot.* But his smile faded when he saw a little girl slump her shoulders sadly and start to walk away. Billy knew what it was like to be a broke little kid with no money for fun stuff. "But, uh," he added hurriedly, "kids under ten are free!"

The next hour was a blur of smartphone flashes, selfie grins, and scribbled autographs. Billy hadn't actually decided on a name yet, so he made sure his signature was just an unreadable squiggle. Finally, the crowd started to thin, and Billy's stomach growled loudly. Time for a cheesesteak. He took a deep breath of crisp Philadelphia winter air. The sky was blue, and the old stone buildings stood against it, looking homey and welcoming. Suddenly, Philly seemed a lot friendlier to Billy than it ever had before.

The scream of car brakes derailed the cheerful thought. A young woman was crossing the street with her nose buried in a letter she was reading. And she was about to be hit by a car skidding uncontrollably toward her! Billy launched himself into the street with his super-speed before he knew what he was doing. He reached her just in time, tackling her out of the way as the car swept by.

"You okay?" he asked, helping her up and dusting her off. The young woman shook her head, confused, and her hood fell away from her face, revealing . . .

Mary! Billy nearly took off running, before remembering at the last minute that he was in his super hero body, and that she had no way of knowing 1) that it was him, and 2) that he was skipping school.

"What—what happened?" Mary said, looking stunned and confused. "You're . . . that super hero? Why—? What—?"

"You almost got hit by a car," Billy said, flustered. "Are you all right, Mary?"

She looked at him, her eyes suddenly sharp and curious. "How do you know my name?" she asked. "Have we met?"

Panic washed over Billy. *Stupid, stupid, stupid!* "Uh," he stammered, "no, just—guessing people's names is one of my powers!"

Mary looked skeptical. Billy plowed on. "So, stranger named Mary," he said, doing his best to look like a grown-up super hero and not at all like Billy Batson wearing a grown-up super hero's body, "are you okay?"

Mary nodded slowly. "I think so," she said. She squinted at him. "Are you *sure* we haven't—"

"Okay!" Billy said, beating a hasty retreat. "Glad you're okay! Bye now! Toodles!" He raced away, leaving Mary shaking her head in confusion at the side of the street.

Billy was having some good, old-fashioned fun shooting lightning from his hands on the steps of the art museum when Freddy found him.

"Lightning! From! My! Hands!" Billy sang cheerfully. "Lightning! From! My! Oh jeez." He skidded to a stop and looked Freddy up and down.

"You look awful," he blurted out. Freddy was disheveled, and his hair was dripping wet. He looked like he'd been beaten up, shoved into a toilet bowl for a swirly, and then locked in someone's locker. Brett and Burke really appreciated the classics.

"This is your fault," Freddy said, quietly furious. "You literally did the *opposite* of what a super hero's supposed to do."

Billy looked around, his stomach clutching guiltily. The small crowd that had gathered to watch his lightning display was watching—and filming—every word he exchanged with Freddy. He cleared his throat and struck a heroic pose.

"I'm a super hero," he told Freddy loudly. "I have *real* problems to solve. But that's a burden I gladly bear, with my—"

He raised his hands back up in the air, and started firing off lightning bolts again. "Hands!" he sang, launching back into the song. "Lightning! From! My! Hands!"

The crowd ate it up, laughing and cheering. But their cheers turned to screams, and Billy turned to look where they were all pointing.

One of his lightning bolts had hit a bus on an overpass not far from the museum steps, and the bus had careened out of control! It had hit the railing at the side of the overpass, bulldozed through it, and now teetered at the edge of the overpass. The screams of the passengers were clearly audible. Just one little shift in its weight, and the bus would come crashing down hundreds of feet to the ground.

Everyone inside would be killed.

Billy watched in horror as the bus started to tip. "Holy moly," he breathed. This was bad. This was Superman bad. But Superman wasn't here.

Billy would have to do.

He used his super-speed to zip over to a spot right underneath the bus. He stared up at it as it wobbled on the edge of the overpass. The screams of the passengers were even louder from here.

"Now what?" Billy said to himself. He looked around, desperate for some piece of inspiration. But there was nothing—and nobody—but him.

"I guess I'm doing this," he said to himself. He opened

his arms, stared up at the dangling bus, and braced himself for impact.

The bus fell.

Inside, the passengers clung to their seats, to the poles, and to one another, as they plummeted. But instead of the crashing *crunch* that they were expecting, the bus slowed and bounced gently.

Billy had caught it.

He crouched, breathing hard, his arms straining, directly under the fallen bus. His fingers dug into the metal, denting and tearing it . . . but his grip held. He'd done it. And now all he had to do was lower it—gently—to the ground. No problem. Except—

He froze. The world's cutest puppy was sitting directly under the bus, cheerfully panting and looking around without a care in the world.

"Shoo!" Billy hissed. "Go! Go on!"

The puppy looked at him and wagged its tail in a friendly way. And didn't move.

"Get!" Billy said urgently. "This bus weighs a freaking ton, pooch!"

The puppy looked away. Billy almost started crying. His arms were trembling, and his grip was going to slip any moment. Inside the bus, he could hear the passengers praying, crying, comforting one another.

Billy held the bus as best he could, but his grip was failing—inch by inch it was dropping lower and lower, toward the little dog. He sucked a breath in and held it.

And then, finally, as Billy's vision was beginning to swim, the dog stood up and trotted away.

"*Thank* you," Billy said, heaving a sigh, and eased the bus down onto the ground.

A huge cheer went up from all around him as the passengers and driver spilled out of the bus, safe at last. Billy looked around—a large crowd had formed and he hadn't even noticed. He felt dazed. Was this what it felt like to be in shock? His mind kept skipping over the moments when the bus was falling toward him. He hadn't been at all sure he'd be able to catch it. But he had caught it.

He *had* caught it! He'd done it! It was his first big adventure as a super hero, and he'd nailed it!

Billy looked around jubilantly. There was Freddy! Good old Freddy. He was coming toward Billy. Billy bounded up to him and shook him by the shoulders.

"Did you see that?!" Billy asked, picking Freddy up and twirling him around.

"Yeah," Freddy said sourly, "you threw a lightning bolt at a bus and almost got a bunch of people killed."

Billy set Freddy down. "Yeah," he said, "but then I caught it. I caught a *bus*, Freddy! Who even does that? I do!"

"You charge people for selfies," Freddy said. "You're the worst super hero ever."

Billy drew back. That kind of hurt. Not that he actually cared what Freddy thought or anything. But . . . well, he guessed he did care. A little.

Billy scowled. Who did Freddy think he was, anyway? He didn't understand anything about Billy's life. *He* wasn't a super hero.

"You're just jealous!" Billy yelled as Freddy walked away.

Freddy turned around. "Yeah, no kidding!" he said. He gestured at his crutch. "I would love to have those powers! And I'd actually *use them for good*."

He looked Billy up and down scornfully. "All that power," he said, "and you're no better than Burke and Brett."

And with that, Freddy stalked off.

CHAPTER 12

Stupid Freddy.

Billy kicked a Dumpster in frustration and then looked around guiltily—the Dumpster was now a crumpled heap.

Whatever. Just because Billy was a super hero now didn't mean he wasn't still human. It didn't make him automatically perfect or something.

"Ah," a weird, grating voice said from behind and above Billy. "The perfect man."

Billy turned. A creepy-looking old bald dude with a glowing eye was . . . flying? Yeah, he was definitely flying toward Billy. He landed gently on the sidewalk in front of Billy and walked toward him.

"The Champion," the old guy said bitterly. "The chosen one. Pure of heart, brave and true."

Jeez. First Freddy, now this dude. What was his deal?

"I want your powers," the guy said conversationally, "and I'll kill you if you don't give them to me."

"Oh, snap," Billy said. "You're a super-villain. Look, before this goes any further, you should know I'm basically invulnerable, so—"

Billy was cut off by a slug to the stomach. The blow doubled him over and sent him stumbling back.

"Ow," he breathed. "How did—"

This time the punch landed square on his jaw, snapping his head back and sending him sailing into a nearby parked car, which crumpled from the impact.

Billy picked himself up. His stomach hurt. His face hurt. And when he touched his mouth, his hand came away bloody.

He looked up at the bald guy in shock. He'd never *bled* when he was in his Shazam body. Not even that time Freddy had put a lit stick of dynamite in his mouth.

"Humans cannot touch our kind," the guy said. "Only magic can overcome magic." He reached out and grabbed

Billy by the neck, squeezing with one powerful hand and lifting him clear off the ground. Billy dangled, gasping and choking and scrabbling uselessly at the guy's fingers.

"*Give me your power*," the man said, glaring straight into Billy's eyes. Billy's vision swam—he might be basically invulnerable, but he still needed to *breathe*, apparently.

Billy nodded frantically. He held his hands up in surrender.

The guy nodded, pleased, and lowered Billy to the ground. "Very wise," he said. He looked at Billy thoughtfully. "You should know the name of the man who has defeated you—the man who is going to strip you of your powers. I am Thaddeus Sivana, and I am— *Ooof*."

Billy sucker punched him.

"Boring," Billy said, finishing Sivana's sentence for him while he was doubled over. Billy leaned back, winding up a punch that he was pretty sure would knock out King Kong. This fight was about to be—

Huh? A blur of motion swept by him, and Billy was yanked into the air.

Sivana had grabbed Billy and was flying him up, up, up, and up into the sky—past the tallest skyscrapers of the Philadelphia skyline, and up through the wispy winter clouds. Soon they were in the thin, freezing air that only airplanes ever saw. The curve of the earth far below them was clearly visible, and there was nothing keeping Billy from plummeting to the ground except Sivana's grip on his wrist. Sivana slowed to a stop and turned in the air to face Billy.

"You will come with me to the temple—to the Rock of Eternity. There, you will give me your power," Sivana grated out, his voice tinny and faint in the thin air. "There, you will submit."

Billy gasped, his lungs screaming. Submit? This guy had to be kidding. Ten years in foster care, exploited by jerks and losers, desperately searching for a mother who didn't want him—if *that* hadn't broken Billy, no way was a rando with a gross eye problem going to manage it.

"Bite me," he said.

In a single motion, Sivana released Billy's wrist with one hand and punched him with the other. The blow was so powerful that it sent Billy rocketing back down toward the earth even faster than he would have fallen on his own. As he tumbled, the air screaming past his ears, Billy tried desperately to focus.

Fly, he commanded himself. *Fly fly fly fly fly!*

He did not fly.

Flyflyflyflyflyflyfly!

Nope.

Billy watched in fascinated horror as the streets of Philadelphia began to get bigger and bigger below him. Soon he could make out trees, cars, people—invulnerable or not, he was going to be a pancake in seconds if he didn't come up with something. But there was nothing he could think of except flying. Which he couldn't do.

He squeezed his eyes shut. If he couldn't fly, then he was going to die, and he didn't really want to watch it happen. Which it was definitely going to, in three, two, one . . .

. . . nothing happened.

Billy risked opening an eye, just a crack. All he could see was . . . pavement? It was about a foot below him.

He opened both eyes wide.

Billy Batson, aka the Pennsylvania Power, aka Lightning in a Bottle, aka Power Boy (*I have* got *to figure out an actual name for myself,* Billy thought), was . . .

Flying.

Well, hovering, really. About fourteen inches above the ground.

"Holy moly," Billy whispered. He'd done it. He'd saved his own life at the last possible second. He looked up to see if anyone had witnessed this latest miracle—with any luck somebody was live-streaming this to Facebook at this very moment!—but what he discovered was this: he was right in the center of the passing lane of Philadelphia's busiest highway, and—

BLAM.

A giant semi smacked Billy straight over the median into the other side of the highway, where—

SPLAT.

A minivan full of screaming children sent him careening through the air. Several more cars and trucks sent Billy's body ricocheting around as though the highway were a pinball machine, and he was a very confused, very frightened ball, until he finally rolled to a stop on the shoulder of the road.

Billy lay there like a beached whale, staring up at the flat gray winter sky. Automobiles tore down the highway a couple of feet next to his head. A faint siren got nearer and louder. A distant crow cawed. And, gradually, Billy's racing heart slowed down enough for him to sit up and then climb to his feet.

He could fly.

He could *fly*!

Now that he'd done it once, he knew he could do it again—it was like it had been in his mind and his body this whole time, but he hadn't known where to look for it.

"I can fly!" Billy said, springing into the air. He soared up five feet, then ten, then twenty.

"I can fly!" he yelled, to the whole city, to anyone who was listening. This was the greatest day of his life! Nothing was going to take this moment away from him!

"I can fly!" he screamed to the sky. "I can—"

WHAM.

Sivana came rocketing from nowhere like a bat out of hell and slammed into Billy, sending him crashing into the shopping mall next to the highway.

Being thrown through several layers of concrete, rebar, asbestos, plaster, and, finally, a rack of women's underwear was not Billy's favorite life experience to date. He sat up, rubbing his head and blinking hard. He was in a women's underwear store. And he could only see out of one eye.

Oh god, he thought, *I've gone blind.*

A young saleswoman approached him cautiously. "Sir," she said, "if you'll allow me—" She plucked something black and lacy off of Billy's head. Suddenly, he could see out of both eyes again.

"Thanks," Billy said, blushing. "Sorry about—uh, everything," he added, gesturing around at the huge hole in the wall, and all the frilly underthings scattered on the floor.

"Oh, don't worry, we have super hero insurance for just this sort of thing," the young woman said briskly. Then she smiled. "I saw you on Twitter. You're Power Boy, right?"

"No!" Billy said. She looked confused. "I mean, yes," he added, "I'm that guy. But my name isn't Power Boy."

"What is it?"

"I don't know yet," Billy said, grimacing. "But don't worry, I'll do an Instagram story or something when I figure it out."

"Speaking of!" the saleswoman said, brightening up. She whipped out her smartphone. "Can I get a selfie before you go?"

Billy grinned. "Anything for my adoring public!" he said. "And no charge," he added, still feeling kind of bad about the mess.

He leaned in and gave a big, cheesy grin as she snapped a pic of the two of them together.

And then—

WHUMP.

Sivana came speeding through the giant hole in the wall and pummeled Billy through another three walls until he landed in the middle of a big crowd of holiday shoppers in the food court.

Screams rang out as Billy bounced and rolled, sending people flying in his wake. This time, Billy was ready. The moment he rolled to a stop, he scrambled under the counter of a Panda Express.

This is crazy, Billy thought, his heart hammering. *You don't have to fight this guy; this isn't your job. You're just a kid. You can just run.*

Billy was good at running. He'd been doing it most of his life.

Over the screaming of the crowd and the pounding of thousands of feet, he could hear Sivana yelling, "CHAMPION! FACE ME!" From the sound of it, he was tearing the mall apart, looking for Billy. Whoever this guy was, he was bad news, and Billy didn't want anything to do with it, no matter how many people Sivana was hurting—and no matter what a super hero like Billy was *supposed* to do in these situations.

Keep your head down, Billy reminded himself. It was a philosophy that had served him well his whole life. *Don't get involved.*

And if he had an ugly feeling in the pit of his stomach, well, it was probably fear. It definitely wasn't shame.

"Shazam," Billy whispered. Lightning arced around him as his body shrank back down to his teenage form.

He stood up, brushed himself off, and slid into the fleeing crowd, slinking out of the mall. Behind him, Sivana roared in fury and tore apart a Panera, looking for a super hero who didn't exist.

CHAPTER 13

Freddy had never been so mad in his entire life, and that included the time one of Darla's classmates had called her a weirdo and made her cry.

He had just watched Billy catch a falling bus with his bare hands—which, okay, if Freddy was being honest with himself, that had been really cool. *But.* The bus would never have been in the air if it hadn't been for Billy in the first place. If Billy hadn't been the worst super hero ever.

I hate him, Freddy thought, kicking a Dumpster. *Ow.* Now his foot hurt, too, on top of everything else. On top of the black eye, and the bruised wrist, and the humiliation of being pummeled by Brett and Burke *again.*

I hate him, I hate him, I hate him, Freddy chanted in his head. But the truth was, he didn't hate Billy, and he knew it. Freddy hadn't made it through years of foster care without learning some ugly truths about himself. He wasn't mad because Billy was an immature jerk. He was mad because he'd thought there was finally something special about him—he was best friends with a super hero! *Brothers* with a super hero. He'd been so excited, but he'd been wrong. He wasn't best friends with Billy—and he *really* wasn't Billy's brother. Billy was as messed up as Freddy was, and he had one foot out the door already. He was just biding his time before he disappeared and left Freddy alone . . . again.

And it wasn't like it was Billy's fault. Billy was just being . . . Billy. He was being stupid and selfish, sure, but that was his problem, not Freddy's.

Freddy sighed. He'd just . . . he'd *wanted* it so badly. He'd wanted a best friend; a super hero watching over him; a reason to think he was something more than just a jittery kid with a highly visible disability, spending most of his time at school trying not to get beaten up.

Well, it wasn't like he didn't have *anything*, Freddy reminded himself. He had his foster family at the group home. He had his sense of humor. And he had his Superman bullet—Billy had returned it to him the night he'd turned into a super hero. Freddy slid his hand into his pocket and clutched the bullet tight. Enough self-pity. He squared his shoulders and tilted his chin up. Billy would have to figure his own stuff out. Meanwhile, Freddy had a life to live.

And there was plenty to appreciate about his life. Even right now. It was a perfect winter day—chilly, but not too cold, and some pretty snowflakes were just starting to fall. There would be snow on the ground by tonight, and it was Mary's night to make dinner, which meant spaghetti, which was Freddy's favorite. Freddy looked up into the sky, taking a moment to appreciate the silhouette of the Philadelphia skyline, the snowflakes drifting down gently, the super hero plummeting to the earth in a blur of red and gold and white—

Wait, what?

Oh god, that had been Billy. How had he gotten so high up? Was he okay?

Freddy watched in amazement as Billy rose up from

the highway and flew—flew!—about fifteen feet up, hovering effortlessly in the air.

"I can fly!" he heard Billy yell faintly, even though the highway was at least three blocks away. Freddy started making his way toward Billy as fast as he could.

"Oh man, oh man, I wish I had my clipboard," he muttered as he shuffled along, never taking his eyes off Billy.

"I can fly!" Billy yelled again. "I can—

Freddy watched in horror as a guy in a dark coat shot down out of the sky and swerved to crash straight into Billy, propelling him off the highway and smashing him through the wall of the mall next door.

This was not good. This was, like, *super-villain* not good.

By the time Freddy made it to the mall, things were not looking so good. Lightning was arcing around the building, and thousands of screaming people were jamming the doorways in their hurry to flee.

"Billy!" Freddy yelled, doing his best to stand against the tide of people without being knocked over. He fought his way inside and ducked into the doorway of an electronics store.

"Billy!" Freddy yelled again, as loud as he could. "Where are you?"

"Yes," a sinister voice behind him said. "Where *is* Billy?"

Freddy's blood ran cold. Very slowly, he turned around. The guy who had punched Billy through the air was standing behind him, a mean smile on his face. He nodded meaningfully at the display of television screens in the window of the electronics store, and Freddy followed his gaze. There, flickering in unison across ten different screens, was a news report showing Freddy and Billy arguing beside the bus accident. Billy's cape was billowing heroically, and Freddy's face was pinched and unhappy.

"So the big red waste of space has a vulnerable little friend," the guy said, prowling closer. He looked very pleased, and that, more than anything else about this situation, frightened Freddy the most. You didn't want people like this guy to get their way.

The super-villain grabbed Freddy by the collar and shoved him back against the glass wall of the store.

"Tell me where the Champion lives," he demanded.

"You should—you should really call him by his proper name," Freddy said, choking the words out around his terror.

"And what's that?"

"Power Boy."

The super-villain rolled his eyes. "Predictably terrible," he said. He dropped his grip on Freddy's collar and grabbed him by the neck, slamming him back against the wall again.

"Tell. Me. Where. He. Lives."

Freddy mutely shook his head.

"Adorable," the super-villain said, and lightning seared through Freddy's body.

⚡⚡⚡

It was Mary's night to make dinner. She glanced at the clock, trying to figure out how much time she had left for her math homework before she needed to go start chopping vegetables for the tomato sauce. She was making spaghetti, like usual, even though she was kind of tired of it. But Freddy and Darla loved it, and Mary loved *them*, so . . . spaghetti. Again.

Snow fell outside the window, making the living room feel even cozier. Mary was curled up on the floor in front of the couch, with Eugene beside her, his nose buried in a book about Minecraft strategies. Darla and Pedro were on the couch, sharing a big fluffy blanket and arguing cheerfully over what to watch on TV. They finally settled for flipping back and forth between two shows, and Mary let herself sink back into the problem she was working on.

"What the heck," Pedro said suddenly, and Mary looked up, following his gaze to the TV. On the screen, a shaky video showed that new Philly super hero arguing with some kid.

Hey, thought Mary, *that's the guy who pulled me out of traffic today.*

"Hey," said Eugene, "that's *Freddy*."

It *was* Freddy. Mary stared at the screen, baffled. What were the odds that this guy would run into her *and* Freddy on the same day?

"What's Freddy doing with a super hero?" Pedro wondered out loud.

Mary's thoughts raced. Something here didn't add up.

And then, suddenly, it clicked.

"Maybe the question," she said slowly, "is, what's a super hero doing with *Freddy*?"

Eugene looked at her blankly. "Huh?"

"That guy pulled me out of traffic this afternoon," Mary said, pointing at the TV. "He knew my name."

Darla gave a muffled squeak and clapped both hands over her mouth.

"And I heard Rosa telling Victor that the school called her today," Mary went on, "to tell her that Billy hadn't shown up for class."

"Wait . . . ," Pedro said slowly. "Are you saying . . ."

". . . that's Billy?" Eugene finished, pointing at the screen.

"OH, THANK GOODNESS YOU GUYS FIGURED IT OUT," Darla blurted out, flinging her arms into the air.

Mary turned and stared at her.

"And you did it all on your own!" Darla said, smiling hugely. "I didn't break any promises or anything!"

"Wait," Mary said, "you *knew*?"

"And you . . . kept it to yourself?" Pedro added skeptically.

Darla beamed.

"I'm such a good sister," she said.

CHAPTER 14

Billy went back to the group home.

He wasn't sure why; at this point it would probably make sense to just hit the road again—run away, live rough for a few weeks while he figured out his next move. But he was so tired. And he hurt all over. And there was something about that place . . . it didn't feel like home exactly, but it felt like it *could* feel like home. Maybe. Eventually. Plus, Mary was making spaghetti tonight, and that was Billy's favorite.

Billy didn't think about it too hard. He didn't want to admit that the word "family" kept running through his head. The fight with Sivana had scared him. His whole body ached. And right now, more than ever, he wanted—

I must be really tired, he thought. He shook his head as he walked, knocking a few snowflakes out of his hair. The snow was still falling, and it had started sticking. A soft, fluffy blanket of untouched snow lay on the ground, and a delicate edging of white lined every tree branch and twig.

Billy turned the corner, and there it was—the group home. The run-down old Victorian looked cozy and snug in the snow, with icicles forming on the eaves, and the windows glowing with warm light.

Billy thought of a line from a poem he'd read in three different English classes in three different schools: "Home is the place where, when you go there, they have to take you in." Victor and Rosa didn't have to take Billy in—but he knew they would. And right now, knowing that felt . . . good.

He opened the door and walked in, shrugging out of his coat and knocking snow from his hair.

"I know it was you," a voice said, and Billy froze. Mary stood in the entryway, flanked by Pedro and Eugene. Behind them, Darla was hopping up and down, trying to peer over their shoulders.

"I didn't tell them!" she yelped. "I kept your secret, I swear I did!"

"Tell them . . . what exactly?" Billy said cautiously. Mary arched an eyebrow.

"What do you think you know?" he asked her.

"You saved my life," Mary said.

Ah.

"Yeah, well," Billy said, his face going hot, "I'm not doing that stuff anymore. It turns out I'm not very good at it."

"I dunno," Mary said, moving aside and gesturing Billy into the living room, "I'm still breathing, so from where I stand, you're doing just fine."

Billy slumped past her. He wasn't sure how to feel about all of this. After the fight with Sivana, he'd kind of decided to just forget about the whole Shazam thing for good. Freddy had had a point: Billy had been handed all this power, and pretty much all he used it for was goofing off. And that really wasn't how a super hero was supposed to act. You never saw Superman, like, juggling elephants just to show off how strong he was.

Mary sat down on the couch and patted the cushion next to her encouragingly. Billy flopped down.

"I'm the worst super hero ever," he said.

"Because of the bus?" Mary asked. Billy looked up, surprised.

"We saw it on TV," Mary explained.

"Because of everything," he said. "But yeah. Because of the bus."

Mary looked thoughtful. "Nobody's good at something new the first time they try it," she said. "Everything takes practice, you know? And some things you just can't do all by yourself. Sometimes you need a team, and that's okay."

Billy rolled his eyes. "Spare me the Self-Help 101, okay?" he said. "I got Freddy beaten up, I nearly killed a bus full of people, and now I've got a freaking super-villain after me. And, by the way, I totally ran away like a coward instead of sticking around and fighting him."

Mary grimaced sympathetically. "Okay," she said. "You suck at this. Point taken. So do better next time. We can help." She gestured at Pedro, Eugene, and Darla, who all nodded eagerly.

Billy shook his head. "There's no 'next time,'" he said. "This was fun, but I'm done with it."

Mary shrugged. "Okay," she said, "I'll let it drop now, but this conversation isn't over." She looked him up and down. "Go wash up," she said. "You look like you've gone six rounds with an angry rhino."

"I *feel* like I have," Billy said, getting up stiffly. He headed up the stairs, lost in thought.

Mary had said, "We can help." Like it was that easy. Like a team—a *family*—was something you could just . . . have. Some people, Billy had always figured, just didn't get to have families. And he was one of them, and that was okay. He was okay on his own. It was probably better that way, he'd decided long ago—if you don't depend on people, they can't let you down.

Mechanically, Billy turned the water on in the sink and started washing his face. The cut on his cheek from where Sivana had punched him stung when the soap hit it.

The thing was, Billy had come back. He'd come back to Mary and Pedro and Eugene and Darla. And . . . and Freddy. And Billy was pretty good at lying to himself, but he couldn't kid himself this time: he'd come back because he was tired of being alone.

He'd come back because of the people waiting for him.

Downstairs, the front door opened and shut with a slam. That was probably Freddy. Billy winced. He really owed Freddy an apology.

He dried his face off and headed downstairs.

"Freddy," he said as he turned into the living room, "look, I'm—"

Billy ground to a halt. Thaddeus Sivana was standing in the living room with Freddy in a choke hold. The other hand was raised high, and an arc of black lightning was shimmering out of it, looping like a lasso around Mary, Pedro, Eugene, and Darla.

⚡⚡⚡

Sivana looked Billy up and down with a sneer on his face.

"So this is what the mighty Champion *really* looks like," he said. "No wonder you act like a mewling, stupid child. You *are* one."

"Billy, I'm so sorry," Freddy said, his face twisted with guilt. "He made me bring him here."

Sivana smiled. It was an ugly smile. "A little electrocution works wonders," he murmured. "Your friend became very cooperative after I ran several hundred volts through him."

Billy stood very, very still. "Let them go," he said.

"Certainly," Sivana replied. "As soon as you give me your powers."

"Fine," Billy said. "Take them. I don't want them anymore."

"No!" cried Darla and Freddy at the same time.

"Billy, you can't!" Freddy went on, struggling against Sivana's choke hold. "He'll use your powers to destroy the world!"

Sivana smiled cruelly. "At least I'll be using them to actually accomplish something," he said. He turned and pushed Freddy into the ring of black lightning with the rest of the kids, and with his now-free hand, he threw a bolt of power at the coat closet door. The door lit up, flashing a sequence of mysterious symbols one after another. When the symbols faded, the doorway flashed brightly and the door swung open. Billy recognized the rough-hewn rock walls on the other side. Sivana had opened a portal to the place where the Wizard had given Billy his powers.

"First things first," Sivana said. He nodded at Billy. "You need to transform into the Wizard's Champion. This will only work if you're actually *using* the Wizard's powers."

Billy thought about refusing. But one look at Darla—trembling with a bolt of black lighting hovering an inch from her throat—convinced him to cooperate. He closed his eyes. "*Shazam*," he said.

Lightning engulfed the house and lifted Billy into the air. When his vision cleared, he was back in his super hero form, tall and strong . . . but he still felt completely helpless.

"Shazam?" Sivana said incredulously. "Seriously? That's how you do it?"

"Hey," Billy said, "I didn't choose it."

Sivana gestured at the door. "Whatever. Let's go, Power Boy."

"Let's get one thing straight," Billy said, scowling. "My name is not Power Boy."

"I've got it!" Freddy cried. Everyone turned to look at him. "I know what your super hero name should be," he explained.

"Dude," Billy said to Freddy. He pointed at the crazed super-villain. "Bad timing."

"I know," Freddy said, shrugging. "But this is too good to wait."

Billy sighed. "Okay, let's hear it."

"Shazam!" Freddy said dramatically, throwing his arms out wide.

Hey, that wasn't bad. Even in the middle of a hostage standoff with a crazed super-villain, Billy had to take a moment to appreciate how perfect the name was.

Shazam, he thought. *Yeah, that's me.*

"Enough of this nonsense," Sivana said irritably. "Everybody through the door. Starting with you, Power Boy."

No," Billy said. "Not until you let them go."

"Hilarious," Sivana said, not looking particularly amused. "No, you idiot, the mutts are coming with us. Hostages, to ensure your good behavior."

Billy's heart sank. But he really didn't have a choice. He looked again at Darla. Her chin was up, and her expression was brave, but he could see her hands shaking. He had to cooperate—for her sake. For all of theirs.

It's what a good brother would do.

CHAPTER 15

Billy stepped through the door first, and Sivana herded the rest of the kids through after him, the loop of black lightning still ensnaring them. Sivana came last, pulling the door shut behind him—and it promptly vanished as though it had never been there at all.

"Whoa," Pedro whispered, staring around them.

"What is this place?" Mary asked.

"This is *so cool*," Eugene added.

"Is this a dragon's lair?" Darla asked. "It's a dragon's lair, isn't it. Oh my gosh, this would actually be really cool?

If we weren't being held hostage by this scary, one-eyed, angry man?"

Freddy didn't say anything, but Billy could practically see his hands itching for his clipboard and pen. His eyes were wide, and he was taking in every detail.

"Tell your fan club to shut up," Sivana snapped at Billy, drawing the noose of lightning just a little tighter around them. Billy caught Mary's eye. She was scowling, but she also looked like she was thinking hard. Freddy, too. They didn't look like helpless victims. . . . They looked like they were plotting their escape.

Don't do anything stupid, he thought, trying to project the thought directly into their brains. *Don't get yourselves hurt.*

Sivana sent them over the bridge one by one, the ancient stone grinding as it rotated through space. Finally, they all emerged into the throne room. The rubble of the fallen statues was still there . . . and so was the Wizard's staff. Sivana picked it up, staring at it thoughtfully.

"I dedicated my life to getting back here," he said, gesturing with the staff at the vaulted throne room. "No one believed me. No one helped. I had nobody—except myself."

Despite himself, Billy felt a pang of sympathy. And it

gave him an idea. Maybe there was something left in this guy that wasn't totally evil—maybe they had more in common than you'd think.

"I know what that's like," he told Sivana. "To feel like you're all alone. To feel like there's this one thing—and if you can find it, everything will be okay. I thought if I could find my mom, everything would change."

Sivana glared at Billy. "Shut up," he said.

"But I was wrong," Billy said. "I know that now. *I* was what needed to change."

"Shut *up*," Sivana snapped.

"This whole time," Billy went on, "we thought we were alone. But neither of us has to be. I've found a family, and you can—"

Sivana snarled. "*I said quiet*," he growled in an uncanny voice. It sounded like several voices speaking all at the same time. They echoed through the throne room. Billy stared at Sivana in shock.

"How did you—" he started, but trailed off as seven silhouettes came streaming out of Sivana. The Seven Sins. They danced around Sivana like shadows cast by firelight. Their faces were horrible—masks of anger, jealousy, sullenness. Power poured off of them, making the air tremble. Just looking at them made Billy feel small and nauseated.

"I'm *not* alone," Sivana said. He smiled—an ugly, twisted expression. "I have seven friends who are here to help me make the world suffer for eternity."

"Geez," Billy muttered. "You don't start small, do you?"

Sivana stared grimly at Billy and held out the Wizard's staff. "Hold the staff," he said, "and say the word, and the Wizard's power will leave you and come to me—where it belongs."

A flicker caught the corner of Billy's eye—the ring of black lightning around Mary, Pedro, Freddy, Eugene, and Darla had faded for a moment. Sivana was so focused on Billy that his attention on the loop of lightning was faltering. Billy risked glancing at Freddy, and he could tell by Freddy's answering look that Freddy had noticed it, too. Mary was looking at Billy as well. Billy nodded at them—they had a plan, without saying a single word. Now he needed to do his part.

"Okay," he told Sivana, putting a sad expression on his face. "I'll do it." He put his hand toward the staff. But then he hesitated.

"It's just . . . ," he started. He sighed.

"*What*," Sivana snapped.

"Well," Billy said wistfully, "I'm just really going to miss these powers, you know? I'm really going to miss making . . . *lightning!*" He flung his arms into the air dramatically and burst into song—"With! My! Hands!"

Bolts of lightning zinged off into the ceiling, bringing chunks of stone crumbling down. One of them hit Sivana on the head—hard enough to distract him even further.

"Stop that!" Sivana yelled. The loop of lightning around the kids had dwindled to the thickness of a wire.

"Lightning!" Billy sang, waggling his hips as ridiculously as possible and waving his arms even more. "With! My! Hands!"

"Gah!" Sivana said, throwing his own hands up over his head as more and more stone fell on him. Billy glanced over at his family—just as the lightning flickered out.

"*Run!*" he yelled, grabbing the staff from Sivana. They scrambled into action, Pedro flinging an arm around Freddy's waist to help him move faster. Billy ran after them, clutching the staff and firing bolts of lightning behind him at Sivana and the Sins as he went. They reached the end of the throne room, and Billy spotted a narrow door that opened into a huge chamber filled with . . . more doors?

The room was narrow but long—so long that you couldn't see the end of it—and the walls were lined with doors from the floor up to the very high ceiling. Grand, wrought-iron doors. Plain, weathered wooden doors. A gate sized for an ogre. A tiny little cat-door-sized hatch. Near the entrance to the room, a door lined with locks and bolts sat next to a pink door with white trim and a "welcome" sign hanging from it. Farther along the gallery, a tattered screen door rattled near a glowing green portal. *This looks promising*, Billy thought.

"*In here!*" he cried, and the kids piled into the room of doors. Billy grabbed one doorknob at random and opened it. "Everybody in!" he yelled just as Sivana and the Sins came skidding around the corner into the room. The kids piled in, and Billy pulled the door shut behind them. It vanished without a trace, and he turned around, panting, to see where they'd ended up.

They were in a courtyard in what looked like a castle. A handful of men and women wearing old-fashioned clothes were sitting around a fountain. One of them was playing a lute. They looked up in shock.

"Hey," Freddy said, waving awkwardly. "What's up?"

"Prithee," an elderly woman said, standing up, "what manner of—"

"POWER BOY!" The enraged cry came from behind them, and Billy spun to look. The door had reopened in empty space and Sivana and the Sins were piling through. "Run!" Billy said, and they took off across the courtyard.

Billy threw a lightning bolt back at the fountain, shattering it and sending a rolling wave of water into Sivana's path.

"Zounds!" one of the old-fashioned people said, falling flat in the water.

Door, door, door, Billy chanted to himself. *Come on, gimme another door.*

And there it was—a glowing outline barely visible in the noon brightness. Billy yanked it open, and the kids crammed through it, emerging into the chamber of doors again.

"Billy!" Mary said urgently. "Pick another door, quick—maybe we can lose him this way!"

Billy nodded and yanked open a giant-sized wrought-iron gate. They hustled through it, and he slammed it shut just as he heard Sivana and the Sins emerging back into the chamber of doors.

They were in a huge room—the entry hall to a giant's house. A chair the size of an elephant loomed near them, and as they ran through the hall they passed a house cat the size of a car. This time Billy knew what to do, and what to look for. *Door,* he thought urgently, and there was that glowing outline again! He yanked it open just as Sivana exploded into the giant's hallway, colliding with the huge house cat. She yowled angrily and swiped at Sivana.

Billy grinned at him, raised the Wizard's staff in a cheerful salute, and pulled the door shut behind him and his family.

Back in the hall of doors, Billy pulled open an *Alice in Wonderland*–style tiny door and everyone crawled through it. The world tilted and shifted as he passed through the tiny door—suddenly, he was falling from a skylight into a pool filled with clear, cool water. Billy hit the water with a splash and came up coughing. They all swam to the edge, where—was that a mermaid? Yes, a mermaid was glaring at them and ringing a small hand bell. A butler appeared, and the mermaid said, "Jeeves! Dispose of this riffraff."

"Yes, marm," Jeeves said, and pulled a large stun gun out of his perfectly pressed black suit jacket.

"Door!" Billy yelped, and a door appeared in front of him. He opened it and pool water rushed into it, sweeping him and all the kids through.

Back in the chamber of doors, Billy shook water out of his hair and looked around. "Did we lose him?" he said, just as a door about a hundred yards away began to open.

"Nope!" Pedro yelped, and Billy grabbed for the closest random door.

The chase went on—how long, Billy couldn't say. They never had a moment to catch their breath, hurtling into one world after another. One door opened into the vacuum of space—Billy had another open within about half a second, that time. Another opened into a strange, alien world filled with sentient sponges. And still another put them in the middle of the stage in an opera house during the final aria—half the audience booed when Billy and the kids appeared, and half of it broke into relieved applause.

They passed through worlds where time ran backward, and worlds where giant mice performed experiments on tiny humans. They barged into a university classroom where two mathematicians were arguing with each other in French. "*Excusez-moi*," Mary said as they ran through, and scribbled a bunch of symbols on the chalkboard. "*Sacre bleu!*" one of the mathematicians exclaimed, staring at the board like Mary had just completely blown his mind. They ran through a quiet forest where fairies flitted from tree to tree and glitter fell from the sky like rain. "Go on without me," Darla said dreamily, only moving when Mary grabbed her hand and yanked. Pedro nearly got left behind in a K-pop music video shoot, Freddy had a nerd aneurysm in a world where everyone could fly, and Eugene was the only one who could navigate them through a world that looked like Minecraft come to life.

But through it all, Sivana was hot on their heels.

Finally, as they ran through a crowd of screaming

teenagers at a 1960s Beatles concert, Mary yelled, "This isn't working!" and Billy had to agree with her. They emerged back into the hall of doors, and Billy looked around wildly.

"We've got to get out of here," he said, clutching the staff and making for the small entrance that led back into the Rock of Eternity. But the rotating bridge that led back to the antechamber was gone—as though it had never existed. They were trapped.

"How did you get out of here the first time?" Freddy asked, and Billy frowned. "I don't know," he said. "I just really, really wanted to be on the subway . . . and then all of a sudden I *was* on the subway."

"So, really really want to be somewhere where you can lose somebody real fast," Darla said.

"Yeah, okay," Billy said, grabbing Darla's hand. "Everyone hold hands!" he said, and the kids all linked up.

Somewhere where you can lose someone, he thought. *Take me there.*

The world went black. And then . . .

The cold air and the chattering crowd and the carnival barkers and the flashing lights and the smell of fried dough and hot cider all hit Billy at once. They were at the gates of the winter carnival . . . the place where he'd lost his mom.

It was definitely a place where you could lose someone.

Billy knew from personal experience.

"Shazam!" he whispered, and he shrank back into his normal, teenage body and clothes in a crackle of electricity.

Freddy looked around. "This is perfect," he said. "It's loud, it's confusing, and it's crowded. We can disappear here."

Billy looked around. "Maybe," he said. He wasn't convinced. Sivana was determined, and he had the Seven Sins helping him. "But what if—"

"If he finds us," Mary said firmly, "we fight him. No more running."

Billy stared at her. "Are you nuts?" he said. "You saw what he can do. I'll fight him if I have to, but I'm not putting my family in danger that way."

Mary folded her arms. "That's the thing," she said. "We're family now. We'll stand with you."

Next to her, Eugene nodded firmly. Pedro slung an arm around Darla, and they nodded as well.

"You aren't alone," Freddy said.

Billy stared at them. "You guys," he started, and stopped helplessly.

All Billy Batson had ever wanted was a family. He'd lost one here at the carnival ten years ago. And somehow, he'd found one today, in the exact same place.

"I—" Billy began, but he was cut off by a deafening roar.

"POWER BOY!"

Sivana, flying at the center of a cloud of swirling black shadows, appeared high in the air above the winter carnival. He shouted down at the crowd, his voice magnified and echoed by the Sins.

"POWER BOY, YOUR TIME IS UP."

Billy looked at his family. Darla, Eugene, Freddy, Pedro, and Mary looked back at him, their faces calm and confident.

"Let's do this," Billy said, and Freddy grinned.

Billy raised his face up to Sivana.

"The name," he yelled into the sky, "is *SHAZAM*."